Invisible Green

The photographer hurried out, pulling his hat low against the rain. Before he'd reached the bus stop, the faces of the Seven Unravellers were already blurring in his memory. He thought of old Sir Tony with the joke knife-handle on his back, and he thought of the faces reacting to it: some shocked, others immediately annoyed at the joke . . .

But one face, for a moment, had registered something else: a German might have called it Schadenfreude, but the photographer had to settle for a "devil grin." One, out of the Seven, had been gloating over the "body" of Sir Anthony Fitch. But which one?

The photographer had no memory for faces.

JOHN SLADEK
Invisible Green

WALKER AND COMPANY · NEW YORK

First published in the United States of America in 1979 by the
Walker Publishing Company, Inc.

This paperback edition first published in 1983.

ISBN: 0-8027-3020-5

Library of Congress Catalog Card Number: 78-68541

Printed in the United States of America

10 9 8 7 6 5 4 3 2 1

The awful Mr Green
Is never to be seen.
Is there a crime?
He's not there at the time.
A death?
He vanishes like breath,
Or blends into the scene,
The awful Mr Green.

PROLOGUE

An Evening with the Seven Unravellers

Autumn, 1939

"LOOK PLEASED, EVERYONE," said the photographer. "Now hold it." Twenty years of shooting brides and babies had made him indifferent to the human face, looking pleased or not. All he asked was a good composition: seven pink blobs spaced nicely over the ground glass of his camera. He ducked under his hood and looked again.

One of the blobs was misbehaving. It fell forward, showing nothing but a bald head. The other six turned to regard it.

"Quiet, please. Sit up straight and—" Something was wrong. The photographer ducked out from under his hood and looked again.

One of the Seven Unravellers—the old geezer with the white moustache—was slumped forward in his chair. The wooden handle of a carving knife stuck up from between his shoulder-blades.

"Bloody 'eck," whispered the photographer.

No one moved. For seconds, the other members of the group sat staring. Then one of then reached over and shook the old man gently by the shoulder. "That'll be enough of that, Sir Tony. We're trying to get this over and done with."

The old man sat up, reached over his shoulder and retrieved the joke knife-handle. With a sweet smile, he said, "Just thought it might help to have a victim in the picture. After all, we are supposed to be a murder club."

The woman in the group was trying not to laugh, now, and the two youngest men were groaning and making faces. Somehow the photographer managed to get them all posed once again.

"Hold it," he warned. A kind of murder club, eh? The photographer fancied a good double axe killing in *The News of the*

1

World himself, now and then, but he couldn't see getting up a club to talk about such things. It took all kinds, didn't it? Here they were, meeting regular in the private rooms above Alberto's Restaurant. If they were all so bloody keen on murder, why sit and rabbit on about it over pricey drinks, with the Eyetie waiters goggling at them? They might just as well nip down the road to the Gaumont and take in a newsreel. Plenty of death there: Spain, Abyssinia, and now Czechoslovakia. Always a bomb-burnt church or synagogue and a long file of hurrying, faceless refugees.

There was something odd about these faces too, now that he noticed them. They didn't go together. The Seven Unravellers might have been an odd assortment of refugees, thrown together by some war disaster. There was something else too, something grim in their faces. He couldn't make it out.

"Hold it." He looked at each face, and tried to match it to one of the names in his order book. The old gent, Sir Tony, that would be Sir Anthony Fitch. The two youngsters must be Latimer and Portman. One was articled to a solicitor, someone had said, and the other reading chemistry at London University.

The girl? Blonde, common-looking (especially in that get-up) even if her name did sound exotic: Dorothea Pharaoh. The middle-aged chap with the Army moustache had to be Major Stokes. And the tall bloke who scowled like a gangster at the camera would be Mr Danby, a police constable. Finally there was the slightly fat, slightly effeminate young man with long hair. He insisted on posing in profile, flourishing his cigarette-holder. His name was Hyde.

"There. Thank you, everyone."

Sir Tony offered the photographer a drink. He asked for a Bass and drank it quickly, while putting on his mackintosh. Gervase Hyde drifted over and tried, for a moment, to engage him in a discussion of photography as Art.

". . . painter myself, you see. So I think I can say with some authority that photography has destroyed the old ego structure, the rigid 'outwardness' of art, and left painting free to explore the plastic forms of the id world."

"Id world?"

"The subconscious dream world, realm of dark fantasies and

deep-seated complexes. Where hate, fear and desire are but the masks of——"

Belching, the photographer picked up his camera case and shouldered his tripod. "If you'll excuse me . . . Bus to catch . . ."

"Of course." Hyde turned to Miss Pharaoh and said, "I was just explaining to our friend here . . ."

Downstairs the restaurant was yellow and warm. The violinist played to the last customers, a young couple who probably wished he'd go away. In the back, an ancient espresso machine hissed and hiccuped. Thinking of the rain outside, the photographer considered stopping for a coffee.

But the violinist was looking at his wristwatch, and a waiter stepped forward to hold the door.

"Good night, signor."

"Good night." The photographer hurried out, pulling his hat low against the rain. Before he'd reached the bus stop, the faces of the Seven Unravellers were already blurring in his memory. He thought of old Sir Tony with the joke knife-handle on his back, and he thought of the faces reacting to it: some shocked, others immediately annoyed at the joke . . .

But one face, for a second, had registered something else: a German might have called it *Schadenfreude*, but the photographer had to settle for "a devil grin". One, out of the Seven, had been gloating over the "body" of Sir Anthony Fitch. But which one?

The photographer had no memory for faces.

Dorothea Pharaoh was about to talk on "Holmes and Deduction". While the young men were arranging chairs, the Major joined Sir Tony by the fire.

"Queer thing, murder," said Sir Tony.

"Eh? How's that?"

"I mean the way it's brought us all together. I noticed how that photographer was looking us over. Must have been thinking us an ill-assorted lot."

Major Stokes looked across the room at Gervase Hyde. "Some of us," he said, "are a damned sight more ill-assorted than others. That chap's actually wearing a velvet jacket."

3

"Yes, but aren't we all a bit—odd? Where else, Major, might one find a London bobby, a solicitor's clerk, a baronet, an ex-Army chap, a greengrocer's daughter and a—a bohemian eccentric, not to mention a chemistry student—all gathered in one room to discuss one subject?"

But the Major was not listening. He had produced his notebook and was scribbling again, as usual. Sir Tony warmed his thin hands at the fire and entertained thoughts of murder.

The Seven Unravellers were as mixed a bag as any group of genuine murder suspects, he had to admit. Their backgrounds varied absolutely, cutting across all lines of caste, breeding, money, even age. Even sex, he added, glancing at Dorothea. Nice little piece, completely wasted on these gawky young men. If he were forty years younger . . . But all they had in common was murder. The great leveller, he thought. The democracy of death.

Though of course it wasn't the fact that brought them here, but the fiction. Murder, for the Seven Unravellers, meant a locked room or a country house surrounded by snow. It meant the secret cipher, the disguise, a subtle poison or a silken Punjab noose. It meant Auguste Dupin (meerschaum and meditation), Sherlock Holmes (dope and deduction) or Father Brown (piety and perception). It meant suspects with false alibis, clues becoming red herrings, and courtroom revelations. It meant the problem of the altered will; the problem of the head which struck the fender; and the problem of that critical moment when all the suspects gather together and the lights go out . . .

Murder meant a game with rules.

A game, thought Sir Tony. *Of course. That's why we all take it so seriously. Each in his own way, we take it very seriously indeed.*

Through half-closed eyes, he looked at the faces of the others, his comrades in pseudo-crime:

Major Edgar Stokes looked like many another ex-Army man of his age, forty. He was plump and pompous, sporting a clipped moustache and a clipped way of speaking. On the rare occasions when he allowed himself more than two whiskies, he turned loud and arrogant, a typical Army bully.

4

But there was besides a strange furtiveness in his manner, decidedly unmilitary. That notebook of his, for example. He was for ever jotting and scribbling in it, but with an air of secrecy. He denied that it was either a diary or notes for a story, yet he never allowed anyone to look at it. If asked about it, he changed the subject.

So much could have been put down to his interest in ciphers and spy novels; he might simply have been a naturally secretive person. But now Sir Tony knew different.

Recently the baronet had managed to get a peek at the notebook over Major Stokes's shoulder. He'd seen a meaningless jumble of letters and figures.

"Looks interesting," he'd said. "Some sort of cipher, is it?"

The notebook had snapped shut with a sound like a rifle shot.

"You shouldn't have looked."

"Come now, Major, there's no great harm. We all know of your consuming interest in spies and secret codes and Eric Ambler novels."

"This has nothing whatever to do with fiction." The Major had peered about, making sure he was not overheard. "This is in the national interest."

"Really? Why not let me in on it?"

"You may well smile. But it so happens that I'm keeping a list of possible foreign agents in London. Red agents. People of East European origin. So-called 'refugees'."

"Afraid I don't follow. Are you with the Secret Service? M.I. 13 or whatever they call it?"

"No, I work alone. For the present. But when Britain comes to her senses and joins forces with Germany, my services will be very much in demand."

"Joins forces with . . . Rubbish!"

But, against all protests, the Major had proceeded to outline his entire mad vision of the New Anglo-German Europe. He was not himself a Nazi—but only because he found that philosophy too "foreign". Anything foreign was suspect. It was, to the Major's way of thinking, basically Communistic.

"If I'm in a restaurant and hear a man order beef Stroganoff, I ask the waiter to find out his name. You'd be surprised how often it's a foreign name. Down it goes in my notebook. For future reference."

"But surely—"

"Not only foreigners, of course. Artist-types. People of *bohemian* tastes, like our friend Hyde. Reds, most of 'em. Doing their damnedest to undermine British moral fibre, to sap our strength. Down go their names. For future reference."

It had shaken Sir Tony badly to find, behind the Major's sober and respectable front, the brain of a dangerous lunatic. Perhaps not dangerous, so long as his lunacy kept to a single notebook. *But heaven help us*, thought Sir Tony, *if Major Stokes should ever attain a position of power. He probably suspects us all. Scribbles down the most trivial things we say. Probably fancies himself a spy in the enemy camp.*

Frank Danby, by contrast, probably fancied himself among friends, which wasn't quite true. A big, violent, short-tempered young man, he might be suited for police duties such as man-handling drunks, but he did not fit in with the Unravellers.

Sir Tony looked at him. Even sitting at his ease, Danby kept his big frame tensed for action. One of his heavy hands was clenched about a glass of stout; the other flexed and made a fist. A Woodbine was jammed in the corner of his mouth and its smoke made him squint, so that he seemed to be scanning the room in search of a victim.

Danby's interest in murder was equally unpleasant. He delighted in sensational news stories of shotgun murders. He told the club members, again and again, of the suicide he'd seen in Limehouse: a Chinese gambler who'd hanged himself. Danby relished every crude detail in his own description of the body. The only fiction he professed to like were American detective novels of the plot-free, violent sort. But his current favourite was *No Orchids for Miss Blandish*, a British specimen containing (by Sir Tony's count) 21 murders, 24 beatings and 1 rape.

Danby had only got into the Unravellers by claiming a certain expertise in police methods of investigation. Now of course they knew it was all sham; he was simply what the Americans would call a "dumb cop", and a "rough customer" besides. He'd gone out of his way to be nasty to every other member, but nastiest of all to Sir Tony. His behaviour was almost beginning to make the baronet believe that class barriers were no bad thing after all. Sir Tony had asked him, finally, if he'd considered resigning from the club.

"I'll see you out first," was the reply.

"What do you mean by that?"

"You're the great armchair sleuth. Work it out."

No, Danby was a bad job, and Sir Tony gave up on him. His real hope for the club's future lay with the other young members, though they probably thought him an old fogy. Derek Portman especially.

Portman was a skinny, spotty youth articled to a solicitor's clerk. Besides honing his already sharp intellect on the legalistic turns of Perry Mason novels, he enjoyed cutting into the legal fabric of other murder mysteries. He liked to speculate on "perfect" crimes where the prosecution's evidence was overturned by an alert defence, so that a murderer walked free from the court.

Otherwise, Sir Tony had to admit, Portman was a bit of an ass, and an ambitious ass at that. Knowing of Sir Tony's wealth, he'd tried worming his way into his confidence, and even wooing his daughter, Pamela. Since Pamela would one day inherit, Sir Tony had lost no time in guarding her against any such unwholesome liaison. A man-to-man talk seemed to have done the trick, and no more was said of the matter. Odd, though, Portman's giving up so easily.

Dorothea began her talk. Sir Tony tried to follow it, but somehow, though he took in the words, the sense of it seemed to slip away from him. Something about deduction and bicycles, was it? These young people were a long way ahead of him, especially dear little Dorothea. Too quick by half, with all of her logic nonsense. That's what came of educating a woman beyond her class. The father owned a string of greengroceries, jumped-up little tradesman wanted his daughter to have an Oxford degree. Shame, really. Sir Tony wouldn't have minded meeting a smart little piece like that at work in her father's shop. Blonde curls, buxom figure . . .

When she'd finished her talk he called her over.

"Explain again, my dear. I'm afraid my foggy old brain didn't take in half of it." He patted the arm of his chair. "Sit here and tell me the story."

She glanced at his glass. "How many of those have you had, Sir Tony?"

Impertinent chit, he thought. "Tell me about the bicycle clips."

"Not clips." She drew up another chair. "Bicycle *tracks*. In the Sherlock Holmes story, 'The Priory School', Holmes looks at a bicycle track in the mud and claims to know which way the machine is travelling. He 'observes' that the rear wheel track crosses over the front. You see?"

"I see only your lovely eyes."

A look of distaste crossed her features. "The point is, it's a false deduction. The cycle can still be going either way. Sir Tony, are you listening?"

The room began its slow spin. He heard rather than saw her get up and walk away, and he heard her speaking to Hyde: ". . . drunk again . . ."

Suppose I am, he thought. *What is this, my seventh brandy and soda? And what of it?* He reached for the glass and upset it. As the room went round again, he saw young Latimer grinning at the spectacle.

Leonard Latimer, the chemistry student, was even younger and spottier than Portman. In fact, Latimer fairly glowed with acne, even when he wasn't blushing. On top of that, he stuttered badly. Sir Tony suspected that both deficiencies stemmed from unsavoury, unmanly habits. Once, while regrettably loquacious in drink, he had told Latimer as much. Shouted it, in fact:

"Unmanly habits, I say! Stop now, my boy, before you lose your wits."

The poor blushing fool had tried to stutter some reply, but Sir Tony had carried on:

"You must get hold of yourself!"

Hyde had said, "On the contrary, he mustn't." So of course the others had laughed, and Sir Tony had made an enemy.

He regretted it, for Latimer had a first-class intellect. One day he'd probably be a forensic chemist; already he seemed to have

8

read all the weightiest tomes on the subject. That was all he read, that and the stories of R.A. Freeman, which were much the same. Stories where a murderer is hanged by the evidence from a single speck of dust.

Dust to dust, thought Sir Tony. Then: *I am getting maudlin, aren't I? Too many blessed brandies. Must slow down, at my age. Otherwise, dust-to-dust for certain. Daresay they'd all be happier with me gone. Gone in drink. Drank himself into oblivion.*

Aloud, he mumbled, "Drinkus, drankus, drunkus."

Hyde looked over. "You said something?"

"Ha! Conjudication of the Latin verb *brandibus muchibus . . .*" Sir Tony Fitch sank back in his chair and began to snore.

"Drunk as a baronet," said Hyde. "I wonder why he does it?"

Dorothea looked amused. "I thought deep psychological motivations were your department, Gervase."

"Oddly enough, I was just thinking of motives," he said. "If someone were to bump off Sir Tony, it's possible that everyone here would have a good motive. The police would have no trouble pinning it on one of you."

"I notice you don't include yourself among the suspects."

Hyde raised an eyebrow. "I? No, I have no motive. I rather like the old chap. Rather a gentle, stupid old father-figure, I suppose. My own father is . . . not a fit subject for conversation. Anyway, the rest of you would all seem to have a motive. I alone have no reason to wish him dead."

Dorothea said, "But that would make you the leading suspect, now wouldn't it?"

"Exactly. If ever I do murder, it will be murder without motive. And that's how I'll get away with it."

"The perfect crime? But why do it?"

He fitted a cigarette to his ivory holder. "For money. The money one of you might pay me to do it. You know, we artists will do almost anything for a generous patron."

She looked into his eyes. "I almost think you're serious."

He laughed, looked away, and tried to cover with an epigram: "Being serious, my dear, is one crime I shall never commit."

Behind them, the Major took it down in his notebook.

CHAPTER ONE

MISS PHARAOH FINISHED addressing the envelopes.

"There. I've not been able to stop thinking about it, ever since I had the idea. Now at least I've taken a positive step." She turned her swivel-chair round to look at Sheila, who was on her hands and knees, polishing the strip of floor near the door. "Don't you think it's a good idea, this reunion?"

Sheila looked up. "I'm just wondering what Mr Hughes will say?"

"Martin? What can he say? It's my money and my house, after all. If I choose to be frivolous for once, he'll just have to put up with it. Have you seen the stamp box? I can't seem to find it."

The young woman replied, but at that moment a jet plane's roar swept all sound from the room.

"Pardon?"

" I said, Mia's probably had it."

Miss Pharaoh turned her squeaking chair again. "Really, Sheila, I wish you'd *try* to keep the child out of my things. Meddle, meddle, meddle—I hardly know where anything is."

Sheila sighed. "I'm sorry, Miss Pharaoh."

"It isn't as though you didn't have your own rooms. Mia doesn't have to go sneaking about in my part of the house, does she?"

"No, Miss Pharaoh."

Dorothea Pharaoh was about to ask her to go and look for the stamps, but something in the young woman's appearance made her change her mind. Sheila Taverner's fat, rounded shoulders were hunched up, and her head bent low over the polished floor, in the attitude of a dangerous bull. One never knew with these fat girls; they seemed to resent the slightest correction. Miss Pharaoh vowed that her next au pair would be older and thinner: one of those Irishwomen who took a pride in their work.

"I'd better go look for the stamp box myself."

"Mia's napping."

" I know. I'll be quiet." Miss Pharaoh made her way past Sheila into the hall, and up the stairs to the top of the house. There Martin had partitioned off a tidy flat, just the size for Sheila and her child. She opened the asbestos-lined door and peered in.

It was plain that Sheila had never developed habits of neatness. The sitting-room was a jumble of toys, shoes, underwear, records and women's magazines—the room of an adolescent. She supposed that Sheila had never really had a proper adolescence. Pregnant and unmarried at seventeen was a poor way to begin adult life. And then her unfortunate brush with the law . . .

The stamp box lay under the sofa, upturned and empty. Miss Pharaoh tried the kitchenette and bathroom, then cautiously tiptoed into the bedroom. From a wall poster, a singer named BILLY PAGE (*and the Footnotes*) leered down at her. There were twin beds, one piled with soiled clothes, the other occupied by the sleeping child. Looking down at her golden hair and eyelashes, Miss Pharaoh wondered how any child as small and guileless as Mia could keep the house in an uproar.

Mia's chubby hand lay on top of the blanket, clutching a trading-stamp book. Miss Pharaoh drew it away from her and opened it. Glued neatly onto the pages were her fifteen pounds' worth of postage stamps.

Martin came to measure one of the door frames, which he claimed was suffering from dry rot. She told him about the stamps.

"Aunt Dorothea, what do you expect? I've told you to lock your desk—and your study door, for that matter." His lean, handsome face looked thoughtful. "I suppose I could get you a good safe at a discount, through the firm."

"A safe! My dear, it's only postage, not philately! Anyway, this is only part of the problem. I'm finding that having an au pair about the house is almost more work than living alone. Maybe I'm getting crotchety in my old age, but—"

"Old age? You're not even sixty!" Martin ran his broad hand down the door frame, then spied a pin on the floor and picked it up.

"Well, I feel old—too old to put up with all their little crises. In the past week, that child has wrecked my bedroom, hidden for half a day in the cupboard under the stairs, teased the cat and marked the wallpaper in the upper hall. And now this!"

He fastened the pin on the back of his lapel. "You hired her," he said. "Why not fire her?"

"I couldn't, and you know it. No one else would take her, with her child—not to mention Sheila's little criminal record. I just thought you might have a word with her about the child."

He grinned. "You've got a notion that because I'm a hard businessman, I'm better than you at speaking to subordinates, haven't you? All right, don't worry." He patted her hand and in the same motion looked at his watch. "I meant to look over the garden before I left . . . Oh, well."

In a moment, she heard him shouting in the kitchen: Mia ought to have been in school this year anyway. Sheila would enrol her for *next* year, and meanwhile *control* the child. Was that clear? If not . . .

Sheila's responses were inaudible; probably she was sulking. Miss Pharaoh felt a pang of guilt at having deputized Martin for the job. *Bully for me*, she thought, and an unwilling one at that.

Of course he must shout at his foremen now and then, but that was "business"; away from his building firm, Martin was the very opposite of a bully: kind, considerate, even—and the over-used word suited him—compassionate.

She glanced over to the mantel, where a row of silver-framed pictures told the story she knew so well: the infant Martin with Fred and her sister Alice, proud parents. Martin in his school uniform, alone in Battersea Park as he would soon be alone in the world. Then Scout Martin and Dorothea, both frowning at the sun and leaning on each other for support. Then a series of Martin growing up: bearded at University, beardless in work clothes, and finally the prosperous young businessman, with Dorothea leaning on his arm.

She leaned on him all too selfishly, she knew, and yet he never complained. Though he had his own flat, a fiancée to look after, and his business, Martin seemed never too busy to help about the house here. Whenever a bit of carpentry or a lick of paint was needed, he came to take care of it. He kept up the garden, ran odd errands like a schoolboy, and even helped Dorothea straighten out the periodic muddle of her household bills. When she'd wanted a car, it was Martin who'd arranged the discount on a sensible little mini.

Nor did his consideration stop with his aunt. Martin spent at least one day a month in unpaid social work, for a charity devoted to helping the needy and lonely. It was a mystery to her how he ever found time for his own business, but he did. With the same energy and cheerful dedication he applied to mending a fuse or digging the garden or visiting the sick, he had created the successful little firm of Martin Hughes and Company, Builders.

She studied the photos again, as though searching for some key to that dynamo of generosity in his appearance. Yet he was simply a tall, rather gangly young man with a long chin. His short-cut dark hair and deep-set pale eyes gave him a look of almost military seriousness belied by his youthful smile. It was hard to believe he was thirty.

What a doting auntie I've become, she thought. *Must be slipping into my dotage.* And her thoughts slipped off into word games, punning her own detested nickname. *Dot, Dot's age, dot—* dowry for the dowager, the age of infirmity, *dot and carry one . . .*

Noticing that she was holding the photo not in a position to look at, but to reflect her own face, she replaced it on the mantel. Why shouldn't she dote? Martin was as near perfect a nephew as an old woman could ask for, except—

Except his puritan streak. Hard work and thrift were admirable in their way, but overwork and cheese-paring were simply ugly. Martin reminded her at times of her own father, labouring all his life under the mottoes "Waste not, want not" and "Mend and make do". In Dorothea's childhood it had always been the spotted tomatoes at tea time, the blemished fruit, cabbages already

13

bitten to lace by caterpillars. Whatever was left from the shop went on the table; whatever was left of one child's clothing went on to the next.

She'd hated it then and she hated it in Martin: "Of course it's your money, Aunt Dorothea, but why fling it away with both hands? A small car is just as convenient as a large . . ."

It was all maddeningly reasonable. True, she didn't need a cook and a maid and a gardener. Sheila, like the mini, was a compromise between Dorothea's dreams of extravagance and Martin's intolerable good sense.

But the reunion—that would be her triumph: a sumptuous banquet catered by professionals, and hang the cost! And she would arrange it all on the sly, before he had a chance to make one of his cutting remarks about the starving millions of the Third World. *She* was starving too—for fun and excitement.

He'd never be able to see that. His idea of fun was more hard toil, a penny saved. He'd even left University because he couldn't stand the waste, the enforced idleness, the clubby frivolity. She supposed it came from being born poor, or else was something in the Pharaoh genes—and yet Alice hadn't been sensible at all . . .

His quick footsteps in the corridor made her instinctively reach for something to conceal the pile of unstamped envelopes. But he came in glancing at his watch, not seeing them at all.

"That's that." He dropped into a chair and started rubbing his chin. "I don't see Sheila giving you any more trouble like that. Made her promise to send the kid to school soon. And now she's steaming off those stamps for you."

He looked at his watch again, and she looked too: a cheap nickel-plate thing with a plastic band. Not at all suited to him.

"I promised to pick up Brenda from her work."

"You run along then, dear. And thanks. You've been a great help, as always."

"Why do you keep so many stamps, Aunt Dorothea? Fifteen pounds' worth seems rather a lot, for—"

"For an old lady who has no one to write to?" she said sharply.

"I wasn't going to say that."

"I'm sorry, I'm being tetchy. But actually I do have a fair

14

amount of correspondence. There's my postal chess, for one thing. Just now I'm playing seventeen games, with people all over the world."

He blinked. "Must cost a fortune. Why not let me post them at work? With the franking machine, I can write it off against business expenses."

"But—"

"Say no more, I'll do it." He stood up, picked up the stack of invitations and shuffled through them. "But these—they're all for London, nearly. Can't you just use the phone?"

Miss Pharaoh felt it was time to confess. "Do you ever remember me mentioning the murder club we had just before the war?"

"Murder club? Yes, I think so."

"The Seven Unravellers, we called ourselves. We met once a month, to chew over the latest murder fiction—Dorothy Sayers, Agatha Christie, Ellery Queen. Good heavens, I must have told you all about it. It's how I came to meet Leonard Latimer."

"Brenda's father? He never mentioned that. I always assumed you met at University. Ah, here he is." Martin put one of the envelopes into his pocket. "No use posting that; I can give it to Brenda. Which reminds me, I'm late."

"There was something else—"

He held up a broad, square hand. "Sorry, but Brenda's waiting. I'll drop by tomorrow to look at the garden, and then you can tell me all about your murder club."

Miss Pharaoh was gleeful, though she avoided showing it until Martin had climbed into his car and driven away. She had tried to tell him, anyway. But now the invitations were on their way.

The sounds of her laughter floated out of the room and through the old house. On the stairs, Mia was so surprised that she let go the cat's tail.

Derek Portman's secretary brought him the invitation. "I didn't know how to deal with this," she said apologetically. "What is it, exactly?"

He took the card and read:

*You are invited to attend
a reunion of*
THE SEVEN UNRAVELLERS
*to be held at the home of
Miss Dorothea Pharaoh*

Reception
Dinner
Reunion Meeting
Entertainment

"I'll be damned!" He made a gesture as though to sail the
card towards his waste-paper basket, then paused. "Perhaps I
will go, after all."

"Yes, Mr. Portman?"

"Yes, mark it in my appointment book. I'll dictate a reply
later." He was unaware that his smooth, tanned face was relaxing
into a childish smile. He read the invitation again.

"Might do me good, seeing the old gang. Bores, all of them,
but still . . . At least I'll have a few good stories for them."

"Yes, sir." The woman wasn't listening, only waiting to be
dismissed.

"How long has it been, I wonder? Thirty, thirty-five years. Not
much water under *their* bridges, I'll bet. Most of 'em probably
growing ulcers in the good old grey world of business. And now
they can revel in an evening of murder again. Glorious! Pity Sir
Tony can't be there, he'd have loved it."

Now the secretary was listening. "Your father-in-law, sir?"

"Yes, he was one of us. I imagine he'd be keen to hear the story
of how I briefed the defence for a few murder trials. One in
particular . . ."

"Which case was that, sir?" she prompted.

"Eh? Oh, that'll be all, Miss Emerson."

"Um?"

Leonard Latimer put down his evening paper and looked up. Someone had kissed his bald spot, and an envelope had fluttered down out of nowhere to land in his lap.

"Love letter," said Brenda. "From Martin's maiden aunt. He asked me to deliver it. Better not let Mum see it, eh?"

"Eh? What is it?" He weighed the envelope on his palm.

"Why not open it and see?" She sat down on the sofa opposite and drew up her long legs.

"Miss Pharaoh, you say?"

"Dad, open it! I'm dying of curiosity."

He opened it slowly, read it, turned the card over to see if there was anything on the back, then read the front again.

"An invitation," he said finally. "I don't think I can go. That must be the weekend of the Brussels convention."

She snatched the card and read it. "No, it's not, it's the week after. Dad, why don't you go? You've talked often enough about the old days, your good old murder club."

He took off his reading glasses and polished them. "No, the idea's silly. Complete waste of time. Your mother'd be bored . . ."

"Mum's not invited. Just the Secret Seven, according to this."

"It's not the 'Secret Seven', you know. It's—"

"I know, I know. Just a joke. How about it, Dad? You know you'd like to go."

"Hm. I won't be rushed like this," he said crossly. "I'll have a think about it." But already his mind was racing ahead to the scene: Seven of them gathered once more, to— *Six*, he corrected; Sir Tony was gone these many years. Died, was it? Or disappeared? Gone, anyway. Good job, too, or there'd be a murder at the reunion. If Latimer had had to face that old bastard again . . .

"I wonder what made Dorothea think of it?" he said aloud. "It's not a bad idea at all."

Brenda had taken down the picture from the mantel and was hunched over it, peering at the tiny, stiff faces. "You all look great—just like a lot of suspects in an old country house murder."

"Thank you very much."

"Oh, you couldn't help it. The creepy clothes, mostly. You were so skinny, Dad."

"Implying, I suppose, that I'm fat now. Which isn't true at all."

"I'll bet you couldn't get into that old dinner jacket."

"Threw it out years ago." He looked down at his paunch. "I daresay I look younger and feel fitter than any of the others, except Dorothea."

She grinned. "But you haven't seen any of them except Aunt Dorothea, have you? Not for years."

"True." He patted his paunch and smiled weakly. "But this represents success. I am, after all, research director of Monoflake. And when we join up with that German firm—well, who knows?"

Younger and fitter. He hoped he was young and fit enough to survive the merger. The German research director seemed half his age, and twice as ambitious. He hoped at least that Brenda would be married and settled with Martin before the crunch came. That way she wouldn't have to share the pinch of his being made redundant, the decline of the Latimer income . . .

"Wait, aren't we supposed to be giving a party for you and Martin that very same weekend? What's Dorothea thinking of, I wonder?"

"Dad, listen: it doesn't matter. Martin and I never wanted it anyway."

"But your mother likes to do things properly."

She handed him the group photo. "Stop worrying, will you? We can do them properly some other evening. Okay?"

But the worries kept coming, all evening. Would he keep his job? Could he really afford to settle money on Brenda, as he wished to do? And what of Vera? She'd been acting so strangely of late . . . Was it a touch of jealousy at Brenda's engagement, just Vera beginning to feel her age—or was it *that* again?

And as he lay awake beside his sleeping wife, the worries multiplied. Would the higher price of Arab oil affect the firm? What about his job? What about the unstable value of the pound in Europe? What about his heart: was this really only a gas pain, or was it . . .?

Gervase Hyde sat at his polished pine kitchen table, staring into a cup of coffee. "It must have been a hell of a party," he said. "Judging by the taste in my mouth, someone's been holding a Black Mass inside it."

The girl, whose name he could not remember, said nothing. She began running something through the blender, and the high-pitched whine seemed to cut deep into his raw sinuses.

"My dear, will you stop that racket? My brain's trying to get some sleep."

"There's a letter for you," she said. The blender continued.

"I don't want a letter. I want a bath. Who is it locked in the bathroom all this time?"

"That Albanian poet. He's sleeping in there."

"But why?"

"Because Peter and Jane are on the sofa. You asked them all to stay the night."

"I did? Who are they?"

"The pantomime horse, remember? They sat on your piano stool and broke it." She poured out a milky green concoction and handed it to him. "Hangover cure. Herbal. Very good for you."

He tasted the mixture, made a face, and wiped green foam from his moustache. "God! That's so bad it must be good." He picked up the girl's hand mirror and looked into it. "God! So's that."

He saw that he was not sixty years and one day old, but a bloated creature of at least a century. The curly grey hair looked lifeless in the morning light, and the skin looked greasy, reptilian.

"Did I sleep with you last night?" he asked.

"Slept, yes."

"Oh." He laid the mirror aside. Slowly, bits of the evening came back to him. The girl—Julie, was it? Gillie?—had been tattooing signs of the zodiac on someone's knee. The Albanian poet, who spoke no English, had been reading one of his poems aloud when the Hon. Evelina Biron fell down the stairs. Then

19

someone had tried to strangle the innocuous young man from the Arts Council, just because he'd remarked that Dali was a good draughtsman. And who was it claimed to have visited Howard Hughes, and to have watched a secret blue film made by Eisenstein?

"It's all too tiresome," he murmured. "I need to get away . . ."

"What was that?"

"I need to get away from all these pseuds. My best work is still before me, I feel sure. If only I could start over—take a fresh view, simplify. I need to invent a new art form, something *direct*."

He opened the envelope and read the card.

Frank Danby's invitation came by the morning post. He found it by treading on it, when he went to take Sheba out for her morning walk. Without opening it, he laid it on the mantel. An hour later, he'd forgotten its existence.

Major Stokes loitered outside the little newsagent's, pretending to read the cards in the window until there were no customers inside. Then he cautiously opened the door and, leaning back to see if he were being followed, stepped in.

"A packet of Pontefract cakes, please."

He paid the woman for the sweets but left them lying on the counter.

"Anything else, Mr. Stokes"

"Er—any letters for me?"

"Just a moment, I'll see." She went into the back. A black youth came into the shop and waited. Major Stokes noticed that the boy stood between him and the only exit. With the woman guarding the back, they'd have him trapped.

The woman returned, holding an envelope. "Here you are."

"Thank you." He took the letter and, without looking directly at the boy, began edging past him towards the door. *Steady does it*, he thought.

The woman called out: "Just a moment, Mr Stokes."

His heart was doing something violent. He clawed at the door handle as he looked back.

She held out the Pontefract cakes. "You paid for 'em. May as well take 'em."

"I—thank you." He stuffed the box in his overcoat pocket and hurried out. All the way home by his usual route, doubling back along a side street he cursed himself for a fool. Now *they* knew that Major Stokes bought sweets at this particular shop. It didn't pay to call attention to his habits, as long as *they* were watching. How easy it would be for them to slip him a packet of Pontefract cakes containing a slow-acting poison . . . to arrange a hit-and-run "accident" on his way home . . .

They'd been after him for years, and so far, he'd been too quick for them. The house was almost a fortress, what with special locks, windows nailed shut and a few other devices to detect intruders. And for this reason, they—Green and his bully boys— were now trying to flush him into the open. Once they got him on the run, it would be child's play to kill him—and who would notice the disappearance of one old man?

Major Stokes unlocked his front door, opened it slowly and looked in at the floor. The pattern of talcum powder was undisturbed. Of course that meant nothing. They were clever enough to sweep up their footprints and put down a fresh powder pattern, weren't they? After all, an organization like theirs, with millions of agents all over the world, wasn't exactly naïve. The NKVD could afford to watch and wait, for years if necessary, until it saw its chance to get him.

When he'd searched all the rooms and checked the locks, he sat down to read his letter.

It simply made no sense. Why a reunion? Why reunite the Seven Unravellers *now*, after all these years? It had to be either an Enemy trick, or a secret message from Military Intelligence.

He took the invitation card into the kitchen and tested it over the gas ring for invisible inks. Then, slanting it to the light, he looked for microdots. Nothing. Yet it must be more than just an invitation.

He sat for a long while, staring at the card without really seeing it. The Seven Unravellers. No possible connection with Green and the other Russian thugs. No possible connection—or so *they* wanted him to believe.

Was it another warning? The old murder club—a reminder of murder? Or were they just trying to scare him, keep him off balance? *Steady as you go,* he told himself. Mustn't panic and run for it now. That could be fatal. Much better to play their game, a waiting game.

Might be a cipher in the message itself, eh? Worth a try. Might be a message from our side. Dorothea was one of ours, almost certainly. She could be warning him . . .

He looked at the invitation again. Twenty-six words in it. Could stand for the twenty-six letters of the alphabet. Yes, of course! Taking his own initials, the real message emerged: *E* was *attend,* and *S* was *Miss.*

"*Attend/Miss.*" Don't attend the reunion! Miss it! A trap—danger! Good old Dorothea was warning him after all.

He took out a fresh sheet of foolscap and began drafting his reply. If Dorothea knew what he knew, together they could . . .

The doorbell rang. Almost automatically, Major Stokes reached for the bottle of heart tablets. It would be Green again, with another ultimatum, or . . . *Steady.* Might be nothing.

He tiptoed into the front room and peered out through a crack in the curtain. He could see the doorstep clearly, and anyone who might be standing there.

There was no one.

CHAPTER TWO

THE WHEEZING VOICE was unfamiliar.

"Miss Pharaoh? Miss Dorothea Pharaoh?"

"Speaking."

"This is—this is *E.S.*"

There was a pause, before she said, "Major Stokes? How nice to hear from you again."

"Shhh! This may be an *open line*."

"A what?" When the voice did not reply, she said, "You received my invitation, then? I hope we can count on seeing you."

"Not sure. Don't get out much, you see."

A mental calculation told her that he was now something like seventy-five years old. His Harlesden address might well be some sort of home for the aged; she hadn't thought of that.

"Not feeling poorly, I hope."

"Fit as ever. Fit as ever. It's not that."

"Is it transport, then? I could have you picked up—"

"No! I . . . Can we talk? Is this a private phone? No extensions?"

She blinked. "None."

"Not tapped, is it?"

Repressing a hoot of laughter, she said, "I don't think so. What's up, Major?"

After a longer pause, he said, "I thought you knew. You of all people. You were always quick off the mark. And trustworthy. Er—you did send me that invitation, didn't you?"

"Yes."

"Good. I suppose Danby'll be there? And Hyde?"

"I hope so," she said. "Are you coming?"

"Not much chance of that," he said, and laughed oddly. "*They* mean it for a trap, you know."

"Who? Danby and Hyde?"

"I name no names," he said. Dorothea could think of no reply to that, so there followed another awkward pause.

"Major, are you still there?"

"Green," he said. "Does the name Green mean anything to you?"

"Like Graham Greene? Not especially."

"Clever, isn't it? Calling himself Green. Disguise by opposites, you see? Green equals Red. Only I've seen through it. That's why they're after me."

Oh dear, she thought. Poor old Major. "After you?"

"I know too much. Know too much. Have to be *liquidated*."

"Major, uh, why don't you come and see me? We could talk this over more privately, and—"

"No, no, too dangerous. They're watching me night and day. Have done for years. I've seen them passing signals. At the cinema, the old cough code. Secret clues in the *Times* crossword. Special handshakes. Spreading the word through their vast network of agents . . . I've seen it all. But now they're after me, understand . . ."

"After you how?"

"Who knows? Untraceable poison. A little 'accident'. One way or another, you'll be reading my obituary any day now. Any day now." Suddenly the voice cleared slightly, so she could almost hear the old man calming himself. "I sound mad, don't I?"

"A bit disturbed," she lied.

"They're trying to drive me mad, that's the game. Destroy my credibility, by a thousand and one little tricks. They steal the milk off my doorstep. They ring the doorbell, and when I answer, there's no one there."

"But that sounds like children." she ventured.

"So the police said. They tried to laugh it off as kids' pranks. But would children come into my house and break things? Would they murder Biscuit?"

"Do what?"

24

"Murder my cat, Biscuit. I buried him yesterday. Would kids do that? No, the person behind it all is Green."

"Who is this Green person?"

"Called on me twice. First time offered me money to take a nice long holiday. Offered *me* money! I refused, of course."

"But why should anyone offer you money like that?"

"When I refused, Green started talking about accidents. How an old person living on his own can slip and fall in the bath. How he can turn on the gas and forget to light it."

"Were there actual threats?" she asked.

"Yes, but nothing I could prove. 'How's your cat, Mr Stokes? I don't see him about today'."

She was no longer entirely sceptical. "Major, you must let me help. Perhaps if I talked to the police—"

"No, it's too late for any of that. If they start poking about, the entire damnable conspiracy will melt away. They'll alert the network and the pack of them will *go underground*. I can't risk that. Promise me you'll say nothing to the police."

"I promise," she said reluctantly. This, evidently, was what came of a steady diet of spy novels. "But is there anything I can do to help?"

"You have my address. Meet me outside the door tomorrow morning at nine *ac emma* exactly. I have a letter for you."

"A letter?"

"Deliver it straight to the Ministry of Defence. Understand? Say nothing of this to the others—our so-called friends. I could tell you a thing or two about them!"

At that moment, as so often on London phones, there was a moment of clicking interference on the line.

"A tap!" he screamed. "They're on to us!"

"Nonsense, Major. It's only—"

"*A Red Tide is rising, rising to engulf us all!* Farewell, and remember my exact instructions."

Farewell indeed, thought Miss Pharaoh, looking at the phone. Too much Eric Ambler, that's the trouble. Still . . .

On impulse, she looked up another number and dialled.

"Mr Phin? This is Dorothea Pharaoh. You may not remember

me . . . You do? Well, I wondered if you might possibly come to tea this afternoon. I have a problem I think may interest you."

Thackeray Phin crossed his long legs, eased the jacket of his dazzling white suit, and looked about for a place to put his sola topi. Finally he laid it on the parquet floor next to his chair.

"Young man," said Miss Pharaoh, "do you always dress like that? Or have you stopped by on your way to the set of a 1930s jungle film?"

He'd been craning round, staring out the window into the lush garden. Now he started, and said, "This? I just threw on the first clothes I could find. Anyway, you English are supposed to be very tolerant of eccentrics, aren't you?"

She poured the tea. "Sometimes. But of course I'm an eccentric myself. One of my peculiar little habits is asking direct questions."

"About my peculiar habit?" Phin laid his green umbrella beside the hat. "But then, we amateur sleuths wouldn't be operationally effective if we didn't ask direct questions. So tell me more about this mystery of yours."

"I'm so glad you said 'mystery'. That makes it *sound* a bit glamorous anyway. But I'm afraid Mr Phin, that you'll find it all rather grim and pathetic." She went over the entire story of Major Stokes, from her first memories of him at the club until today's phone call.

He studied her while she spoke. Miss Dorothea Pharaoh was a dumpy little woman with untidy white hair, and a general air of carelessness about her appearance: the brown knit suit and black suede court shoes could not have been put on with any idea of vanity in mind. Pedagogy was the effect, and dullness.

With her face, it was different. Stark intelligence was relieved by the laugh-lines round her eyes. He could see how the lines had developed, for when she occasionally slipped away from the subject to make a play on words, she grinned charmingly, displaying a gold eye-tooth.

He knew Miss Pharaoh only through correspondence. While

he'd been teaching at an American university, they had begun a game of postal chess. Later there had been an exchange of little logic problems and puzzles. When Phin had moved to London, she'd written inviting him to tea "sometime". Now, three years later, he was taking up the invitation.

She finished her account. "I thought of you at once," she explained. "Of course I'm a bit of an amateur sleuth myself, but you, I believe, actually leave your armchair and go out to solve cases."

"I'm not sure I could solve this," he said. "It intrigues me, of course. And yet . . ."

"The spy business sounds bogus?"

"Yes. Could this major of yours really be mixed up with spies? The odds against it are pretty high. How often do Russian agents go about threatening seventy-five-year-old pensioners?"

"Then you won't help?"

"Then I will. I think there might be something more down-to-earth behind it. Such as a winkling landlord."

"A what?"

"Your jargon, not mine. You know what winkling is—digging a winkle out of its shell. And as I understand it, London is full of landlords doing much the same to tenants. Usually these are old-age pensioners who are paying very low rents, fixed by law. And by law, the landlords can't get rid of them. So they bully, bribe, threaten and coerce. There are cases in the papers almost every week, didn't you know?"

"I had no idea," she said slowly. "Disgusting! And you think that's the answer?"

"I've no idea. We don't even know yet if Major Stokes rents his house or owns it. We'd have to find that out first."

"But there's so little time," she said. "That letter of his—it worries me, for two reasons."

Phin made a gesture, almost upsetting his cup of tea. "I think I know them," he said. "If the letter's based on any reality, it could cause trouble with this Mr Green character. If not, the police might hand it over to the health authorities and have the Major put away."

"Exactly. So I want to see that letter, whatever's in it. And perhaps I'll have to hand it over to the police, perhaps not."

Phin started getting to his feet. "Well, then, you've got no problem. Just collect it, as you agreed to do. You won't need me."

"Wait. I shall need you, to find out what's behind it all. I want you to find this Green—who he is, what he does, and why he should be making threats against the Major."

Phin sat back and grinned. "I was hoping you'd say that."

"I do say it, Mr Phin. You must know by now that I can't resist a mystery of any kind. I know you're the same: it's why I decided to hire you."

"Hire me? And wreck my amateur standing? No, you can pay my expenses, but no more. That way I can quit whenever I get bored with it. Now the first step is for me to find out about that house. Give me the address and show me a telephone."

"Then you are interested?" The short, white-haired lady picked up an old black man's hat and flung it in the air, then clapped it on her head. "Oh, Mr Phin! You should have been a charter member of the Seven Unravellers!"

"Thank you."

"I have a hunch this'll be interesting! *Sinister!*"

Phin shrugged. "You know what I always say about hunches, though. What's the hat?"

"This?" She took it off and looked at it. "Just an old second-hand hat Martin bought me for my gardening. Right size, too. Not that I ever do much gardening—Martin takes care of everything. But what is it you say about hunches? You think they have no place in detection?"

"I think not. A hunch, my dear lady, is what one gets in one's back, from carrying a great load of sh——, of useless information."

She howled with laughter, perhaps partly at his fastidious translation.

A few minutes later, when Phin returned from the phone, he was no longer smiling.

"Someone I know at Scotland Yard has checked the address,"

he said. "The Major doesn't live there." He bent down and retrieved his sola topi.

"I don't understand."

"It's an accommodation address. A newsagent and tobacconist who accepts letters for people who don't live there. Didn't he tell you where he really lives?"

"No. Perhaps he means just to meet me at this shop."

"Hmm. I'll see you there, then, at nine sharp. Just now I'm going home to work on something else. Meanwhile, remember what the Major said. Tell no one—least of all any of the old club."

"Mr Phin, do you know something you aren't telling me?"

He looked embarrassed. "No. I know nothing. Nothing at all."

As quickly as possible, he took his leave and returned to his flat in Kensington. He changed into dark clothes and sat leafing idly through an Egyptian grammar until the phone rang.

"Phin? Gaylord here."

"Yes, have you got it?"

There was a pause, then a sigh. "All right. The address is No. 44 Tennyson Avenue, N.W.10. A rented house. Got that?"

"Yes, thanks, Inspector."

"Phin, since I'm breaking the rules telling you this, I think it's only fair you tell me what's going on. Do you think there's a serious threat to this old guy's life, or what? If you do, it's your duty—"

"I don't know any more than I've told you already. Major Stokes is a classic paranoiac so far, nothing more. All the same, he mentions too many genuine-sounding details: I can't believe he imagined them all. So I very much want to see that letter. And to see it, I'll have to protect him long enough for him to write it. I intend to watch his house tonight. That is, unless the police would like to watch it for me?"

"Not a chance of that."

"I thought not. Goodbye, Inspector."

"Chief Inspector, if you don't mind."

"Goodbye, Chief."

Phin drove his hired car through a factory district of the future: famous brand names appeared in lighted letters fifty feet high on large, antiseptic structures set back of well-manicured lawns. Beans, biscuits, boxes, bedsprings and bunion remedies—almost everything "essential" to civilization seemed to be manufactured here in these great windowless buildings.

He drove on over a bridge spanning a canal and a railway line, and the picture changed. It was as though he'd moved back in time. The streets were cobbled, and of the same colour as terraces of squat brick dwellings which lined them: the colour of old brick, coal smoke and poverty. There were broken pavements and pot-holes along every street, and the curious little cast-iron street lamps, set upright in the days of gaslight, were now leaning at crazy angles and shedding a weak electric glow. Many shed no light at all; their bulbs has been smashed, possibly by the hordes of children playing soccer on the cobblestones.

Twilight was the right time to see it all, he thought. It was hard to believe that this depth of poverty existed, and not in a mining town of Victorian days but in London, in the days of Concorde and colour TV. Worse, whoever had built the district had, with a fine sense of irony, named every street after a poet. Phin made his way from Keats Road to Coleridge Avenue, from Byron Street to Wordsworth Crescent, through the poets' corners of Elysium.

He parked in Tennyson Avenue and began his vigil. No. 44 looked only slightly more derelict than the other houses. From the ground-floor window, faint yellow light leaked out round the edges of a shabby curtain. Out front, in the fading twilight, a black and white cat was trying to work its head under the ill-fitting lid of a dustbin. The lid finally clanged to the ground. Almost instantly, the window light went out.

A moment later, it went on again. Now the curtains had been adjusted better.

Before it was completely dark outside, the front door of No. 44 opened. Phin caught a first glimpse of the occupant, a bald, skinny little man in a striped shirt and braces. The man looked both ways, then quickly set out an empty milk bottle and retreated.

For some time after the door closed, Phin could hear the rattle of bolts and chains.

By now the street was quiet. Major Stokes's light went out. In the distance, Phin could hear railway equipment creaking and clashing in the goods yard. For a time, a burst of West Indian music echoed from the other end of the street. At ten o'clock, a car arrived at No. 52, dropped off a young girl, and raced away sounding its musical horn: "Colonel Bogie". Just after eleven the street came awake for a few minutes, as cars driven either fast and erratically, or with suspicious slowness, signalled the homecoming of the pub crowd to houses all along the way. By half past eleven it was quiet again, except for a pedestrian couple, stumbling along the broken pavements and singing "I Get a Kick Out of You".

For the rest of the night, Phin had nothing to do but peruse, by the failing light of a pen torch, his Egyptian grammar. When the battery finally gave out, he turned to his pocket calculator, beginning by figuring his bills, and ending by finding a way to obtain the number 57718 (so that he could turn it upside-down and read BILLS).

Watching a house all night was not Thackeray Phin's idea of detective work. A good sleuth, he often reminded himself, ought to be able to leave work like this, as well as following suspects and grovelling for clues, to the police. A good sleuth ought to be able to sit in an armchair at home and brilliantly guess all the right answers. Sherlock Holmes would never have wasted a night on a pointless expedition like this. Father Brown would have strolled on the scene at nine in the morning, after a good night's sleep, and instantly solved everything. By sunrise, Phin was cold and weary, and feeling sorry for himself.

Dawn was marked by a chorus of sparrows, the slow, whining progress of a milk float, and first signs of life in the houses. The occupant of No. 44 had not yet come out for his milk when, from other houses, coughing factory workers emerged to drive off in their coughing cars. At eight o'clock, the postman passed. By eight forty-five, women were beginning to wheel push-chairs and prams out of their narrow front doors, and off towards the shopping district. By nine-fifteen, there had been a sign of life from every house in view except No. 44.

Phin went to the door, slowly, trying to rid himself of the feeling that somehow he'd been watching the wrong house all night. There was a doorbell and a knocker; he tried each in succession, then both together. When the sound of the knocker echoed away down the street, there was absolute silence.

He looked in through the letter-box slot, then called through it.

"Major Stokes? Hello!"

He peered in again, finally, with more care. The hallway was dim, but when his eyes became accustomed to the gloom, he saw there was a kind of weak light. Probably a hall light, left on all night. He could see a partly open door, and a shadow at the bottom of it. After a few seconds, the shadow became clear. It was a narrow foot in a carpet slipper.

"All right, sir, you keep clear and stay out here." The policeman rushed at the door and threw his weight against it.

"Christ!"

He rebounded, rubbing his shoulder. "Didn't even budge. He must have a bar across that." He stood back again, rushed, and kicked at the middle of the door. Wood splintered and the door flew back.

Phin did not stay outside. He watched the constable's feet move through a film of white powder on the worn lino, leaving the only set of footprints in the narrow hallway. Then he followed him inside. Mildewed wallpaper, a cracked newel post, and the partly open door. The policeman opened it further, and they looked in.

The old man wasn't lying on the floor, exactly, because there wasn't enough floor to lie on. The room was a hall toilet. The old man was thin enough to have squeezed himself down beside the toilet itself so that he was sitting on the floor. The gaudy stripes of his pyjamas accentuated the position of his limbs: one leg drawn up, the other thrust out to keep the door open. His hands were clutched to his chest, but oddly, with the palms turned out as though pushing someone or something away. His bald head was hard back against the wall, his eyes open, and on his face an expression that made the policeman say "Christ!" again. He felt for a heartbeat, but the body was quite stiff and cold.

Phin knew he'd be chased out at any second, so he looked about the room. There seemed to be no marks on the body, but the fingertips were odd: broken nails and dried blood under them. The door had been closed with a simple hook, which had been fastened and then pulled loose. The walls were covered with old, flaking paint, and some of this had been rubbed loose and scattered over the corpse. The toilet had no window, only a small vent.

"Clear out of here, will you?"

Phin walked outside. In the brilliant morning sun, the street and houses looked almost clean. Some kids were out on the cobblestones already, keeping one eye on the police car as they kicked at a football. Phin felt like kicking himself.

"It's good to be alive, isn't it?" he murmured. "Even a frightened old man would enjoy a morning like this, when he steps out to get his milk. Better to be alive and old and frightened than—than that piece of garbage in there. God!"

"Say something, sir?" said the policeman behind him.

Phin lapsed into silence, but he couldn't stop his thoughts: *Poor old man. He was right all the time.*

33

CHAPTER THREE

"MURDER?" Chief Inspector Gaylord tried to arrange his face in a smile, and failed. Other than a slight adjustment of the aquiline nose, a slight deepening of the lines by his mouth, nothing happened on that granite landscape. "You amateurs amuse me. It always has to be murder, doesn't it?"

"Not always," said Phin. "But this time—"

"Is like a thousand other times. It's not exactly rare for a man over seventy years old to keel over with a heart attack. We see a few hundred such deaths every year. And how many old men get murdered every year? Less than a dozen."

"This year you might just make it a baker's dozen. There's something *abnormal* about the death of Major Stokes, and all the statistics in the police computer won't make it normal."

Gaylord turned, twitched the cord of his venetian blinds. Bars of afternoon sun fell across his desk, striping the cardboard file of STOKES, E. W. "Statistics can be useful, Phin."

"As long as we don't worship them. Stokes can't be a useful number, not all by himself. And he *was* by himself, that's the point."

"I don't follow."

Phin sat back, shading his eyes from the light. "I mean, he was a lonely, frightened old man. He thought someone meant to kill him, and he asked for help. And help came—*just too late*. It makes me wonder what was in that letter of his."

"Oh, we've seen the letter. Nothing of value there, believe me. Of course we passed it on to the MoD, but it's completely insane.

"Phin, no one wanted to kill the old guy, can't you see that?

34

He just happened to be crazy, and he just happened to die. Can't you let it alone?"

"Not until I'm as well satisfied as you appear to be. You seem to have it all worked out, on the basis of finding a bottle of digitalis—"

Gaylord jumped as though stung. "How did you know that?"

"I deduced it. You say he had a heart attack, but the pathologist's report can't be ready yet. So the only evidence you can have is the police surgeon's guess, backed up with something more substantial: a bottle of medicine.

"Kind of obvious, isn't it? And what bothers me is, it would be just as obvious to a possible murderer. Stokes claimed that someone broke into his house, some time ago. Such a housebreaker would have had a chance to see his heart medicine and work out a way of killing him."

Gaylord tried to smile again. "You're not suggesting one of those strange and subtle poisons that keep turning up in detective stories?"

"No, nor a hypodermic injection of air, thanks all the same. No, I suggest only that it's easy to kill a heart patient and make it look natural. A bad shock, for instance. The killer gets into the house and—"

"Stop right there. No one got into that house last night. We went over it thoroughly, I don't mind telling you, and it was *sealed*: the front and back doors were locked and chained and barred. Every single window was nailed shut with ten-penny spikes. The passages were strewn with talcum powder to show footprints. There were threads strung across one or two steps on the stairway. There's paranoia for you: the old bloke had turned that house into a fortress. No chance of entry at all."

"How about that little vent in the toilet? That was open."

Gaylord shook his head. "It was also four inches by five. I couldn't put my head through a hole like that."

"But you could put your arm through it. You could perhaps reach a pillow in to smother—"

"Forget it. You'd need an arm eight foot long. Even then

Stokes could have wriggled away and simply walked out of the room."

Phin was silent for a moment. "You're right, I guess. And yet . . . There was a struggle of sorts, wasn't there? A lot of dried paint knocked off the walls. And Stokes's fingernails were broken and bloody."

"Easily explained. The old man had an attack, struggled a bit, and clawed at the walls in his death throes. That wouldn't be unusual either. No doubt the pathologist will find traces of dried paint under his fingernails. Next question?"

"The time of death," said Phin.

"Sometime before two a.m., as near as we can tell. Why? Are you suddenly going to remember you heard a cry for help?"

"No, I didn't. I don't suppose I would have heard him, since the toilet's in the back of the house and I was out front. But that's why I thought of smothering." He brought out a large magnifying glass and used it to study the motes dancing in a sunbeam. "What was he doing in the toilet at that hour, anyway?"

"Believe it or not, we even have the answer for that. Besides his heart medicine, he also had something for his bladder. What's more, I've talked to his doctor, who says it wouldn't be unusual for him to have got up two or three times in the night. Especially if he were worried and not sleeping well."

Phin sighed. "That seems to be that. Er—I don't suppose you've turned up anyone who would have wanted him dead?"

"No. He had no living relatives and no money. The neighbours hardly knew him. As for your international Communist conspiracy, how likely is it that spies would be after a lone paranoid pensioner? He hadn't an enemy in the world—or a friend, either."

"I wonder . . . Could I have the name of his landlord?"

Gaylord looked startled. "His landlord? Phin, that doesn't make sense. What could his landlord know about this?"

"I don't know. If he turned out to be a man named Green, at least I'd have something to go on."

"Meaning you've got nothing now—not a scrap if evidence pointing to murder. Phin, why not be sensible and admit defeat? Green is a figment of the old boy's imagination, and you know it. You don't seriously suggest that a landlord would murder his tenant?"

"No, but I suggest that he might harass him, try to drive him out. And maybe the harassment went too far—I don't know, but I'd like to see the landlord."

The policeman snorted. "You're tired, Phin. And if you don't mind my saying so, the whole idea of an amateur sleuth is pretty tired as well. Still, if you want a straw to grasp at, here it is." He opened the file and turned pages. "The Dartleford Estate Agency. Their office is in Kensington."

"Thanks." Phin stood up and stretched.

The irony in Gaylord's voice was unmistakable. "Oh don't mention it. And *good hunting*."

Miss Pharaoh's voice sounded ruffled. "But surely the police must see what an extraordinary coincidence it is."

"They don't seem inclined to dig much deeper. The question is, should I?"

"Of course, Mr Phin. I hope *you* don't think it's hopeless?"

"I want to go on with it, at least until the inquest. If they find natural causes, maybe we can think again. Just now I'm going to see the Major's landlord. Then I'd like to talk to the other members of your little club."

"Shall I call a meeting?"

He considered it. "Not yet. I'd like to approach each of them indirectly. That's another coincidence that bothers me: if this is murder, it's an almost perfect crime—certainly worthy of someone in your little murder club."

There was a long pause, during which the telephone line buzzed and chattered. Somewhere in the system a crossed line yielded up a ghostly voice: "*. . . looks better since she had her hair fixed . .*"

Miss Pharaoh said, "One of the Seven Unravellers? I kept thinking about that this morning, while I sat in that taxi outside the newsagent's—waiting for news, appropriately enough. I kept remembering how we all really despised the poor man. What if one of us hated him enough to . . . And when it got to be

37

ten o'clock, I *knew* something dreadful had happened. Then that young policeman came to say I was wanted at the mortuary—it was like a nightmare coming true. Or, Mr Phin, we must do something!"

"Because he was your old comrade?"

"Not at all." Her voice sounded oddly elated. "Because it's such a fascinating *puzzle*."

Dartleford was either a very new firm or one which had recently undergone cosmetic surgery. The office, tucked into a street of small, unimposing shops, glittered like a diamond in an ash heap. Chrome letters four feet high proclaimed its new name, DART ESTATE, above a broad front window of blue glass. Inside there were deep carpets, white desks, apricot-coloured phones and of course canned music. The staff were young and glittering too: Phin was passed from a pretty blonde receptionist to a smooth, well-tailored young man, Mr Mock.

"It's one of our Harlesden properties you're interested in, Mr Phin?"

"That's right. No. 44 Tennyson Avenue."

With an obvious enjoyment of protocol, the young man picked up his apricot phone and buzzed a desk a few yards away. "Miss Forbes, could I have the file on No. 44 Tennyson Avenue, please?"

Phin watched her get up, walk to a large circular filing system, and extract the document.

"Oh dear," said Mr Mock, scanning it. "There is a problem. We seem to have a sitting tenant in that house. So we haven't been offering it for sale."

"The tenant died yesterday," said Phin. "I happened to hear about it, so I thought I'd ask. Will you be selling it?"

"We may well consider selling it, Mr Phin. Um, perhaps I'd better put you on to our Mr Bunyan. He's more familiar with this sort of thing."

After more protocol, Phin moved to the obviously superior desk (two telephones) of Mr Bunyan, a slightly older and coarser executive.

"Have a chair, Mr Phin. I must say you're an early bird. I gather you heard old Mr Stoker was dead, and you nipped right round to us, eh? Quite right, too. With the property boom going the way it is, you can't be too quick."

"I believe his name was Stokes."

"Stokes, Stoker, same difference. What matters is, he's off our hands. Have you any idea how much money we lose on sitting tenants? It's criminal, Mr Phin. *Criminal*. We're well rid of him, I don't mind telling you." Something in Phin's face must have registered, for Bunyan immediately added, "Though of course it's too bad he had to pass away—not a relative of yours, I trust?"

"I never met the gentleman." Phin glanced away from the glitter of Mr Bunyan's gold cuff-links. "I suppose sitting tenants can be quite a nuisance."

"Nuisance? You must be joking. They're a dead loss. We can't raise their rent or evict, so we're simply stuck." Mr Bunyan turned his attention to the file in his hand. "Tell me, were you thinking of just the one property?"

"I'm not sure yet."

"Good. Because we can offer a very attractive little package, shortly. Eight houses in the Harlesden area including this one, for say, two-fifty thou. Or forty apiece, say, break it down any way you like."

"Seems a bit steep. After all, I've seen the house, and—"

"Wait, there's more. We mean to convert each house into two flats, before completion. So what you get is a guaranteed income of twenty thou per annum. How does that sit with you?"

Phin pretended to think it over, haggled awhile, and finally said he'd talk to his banker. There was certainly motive enough here, in this high-powered casino of an office. It was hard to relate this glittering place to the crumbling squalor of Tennyson Avenue, but one thing was certain: the death of one penniless old man had made it possible for Dartleford to attempt a deal worth a quarter of a million pounds.

As he shook hands, Phin said, "By the way, I wanted to have a word with someone else here before I left. About another little matter."

"Fine. The office is at your disposal, Mr Phin."

"I wanted to see your Mr Green."

Bunyan was disappointingly calm. "We don't have a Mr Green. Sure you've got the name right?"

"Green. I'm sure it's Green. A friend of mine told me he could put me on to a very good deal."

Evidently this was a false step. Mr Bunyan said coldly, "I don't know who your friend is, and for that matter, I don't know who you are, but we've *never* had a Mr Green working here."

Phin walked to the door, feeling that Mr Bunyan was watching his every move. When he looked back, the feeling seemed foolish. Mr Bunyan, having swivelled round the other way, was only sharpening a pencil over his waste-paper basket.

CHAPTER FOUR

THE SECRETARY WAS FIRM about it. "I'm sorry, Mr Phin. No one can see Mr Portman without an appointment. And I'm afraid he's booked up for the entire day. In fact, I don't see how we could possibly fit you in before Tuesday week. Would that suit?"

"It would not suit. This is urgent. If I don't see him this morning, there's no point in seeing him at all."

The secretary's expression did not change. "If it's that urgent, I suggest you try another solicitor. The Law Society can give you a list. Or why not try the Law Centre, just up the road? They can give you free advice any time. Just join the queue." Her eyes added that she thought it might do him some good, queueing. Impatient Americans needed to be taught how to behave in a civilized manner, waiting their turn.

"It's Mr Portman I've come to see," he said.

"*Sorry.*"

"Maybe I'd better tell you, then." Phin leaned over her desk and tried what he hoped was a mafia leer. "Listen. I've come from a certain client," he said softly. Hoisting his heavy briefcase on to the desk, he patted it. "The tapes. You know?"

"No, I don't know," she said. "Perhaps you'd better give me the name of this client and state your business."

"Huh-uh. Nope. I've got my orders, miss. I talk to the mouthpiece himself, or nobody." He leaned further. "Don't make me do something we'll all regret."

"Is that a threat?"

"Not at all. But if I walk out of here, nobody'll ever hear these tapes. I said it was urgent."

41

A few minutes later, he was shown into Mr Portman's panelled office. The general effect of elegance was marred by the window whose lower pane had been replaced by a large square of cardboard.

"Take a seat, Mr Phin. With you in a minute." Portman was a large, round-faced, healthy-looking man in his fifties. His dark hair, going white at the temples, was brushed back over his ears in neat waves. The hair, with his quietly elegant suit, marked him as a stereotype solicitor: reader of *The Times*, golfer, member of the Conservative Club, commuter from the suburb on whose local Council he serves. But his face was too jolly, too animated for a lawyer's face—and too big. It was the face of an entertainer. Phin had seen such a face peering out from under the jaunty brim of a butcher's straw hat, once, a butcher widely esteemed for his knack of telling coarse jokes to the housewives, making them scream with laughter over the sausages.

Portman made a few notes with a silver pencil, then sat back. "Suppose you tell me about these mysterious tapes," he said. "You've certainly aroused Miss Emerson's curiosity."

"Yes, how else could I get to see you?"

"See me about what, precisely?"

Phin cleared his throat. "It's a personal matter. I believe you're a member of a club called the Seven Unravellers?"

Portman looked slightly surprised, but said nothing.

"I wonder if you'd mind telling me a bit about this club. Have you been in touch with any of the other members lately?"

"What is this, Mr Phin? Just who are you?"

"I'm a private investigator. I'd rather not say who my client is, for the moment, but . . ."

"In that case, I can't help you. Goodbye."

"In that case, my client is Miss Dorothea Pharaoh."

"The devil! Why should Dorothea hire someone to check up on me?"

Phin sighed. "Maybe I'd better start by telling you what I know, and then see what you'd like to add. You know about the coming reunion, of course. Were you planning to attend, by the way?"

"Possibly. Go on."

"Well, Major Stokes won't be there. He died rather suddenly, night before last."

"Did he now? Poor old bugger." After a moment Portman added, "Did you say 'suddenly'?"

"The police are looking into it. There were threats, evidently."

"I see. Is murder suspected?"

Phin shrugged. "I'm just collecting background information, really. What can you tell me about the Major?"

"Why should I tell you anything? Oh, very well, very well. It's going back some time: when I first knew him in the Unravellers, he was fortyish, a bachelor and an ex-officer. Very much the ex-officer, if you follow me. Stiff, humourless, absolutely uninterested in anything but war and spying. He was always theorizing about alliances and secret treaties and arms deals—that kind of thing. A bit of a crypto-Nazi, if you ask me. He always said we'd gone into the Second World War on the wrong side. He was fiercely anti-Soviet, and always talking about communist infiltrators in our midst.

"I suppose he was harmless, really. Somehow he reconciled his views with those of his King and country, enough to reactivate his commission. Anyway we dissolved the club in 1940, and I never saw him again."

The intercom buzzed, and an electronic version of the secretary's voice reminded Portman that he had an appointment in ten minutes' time.

"Thank you, Miss Emerson. I'll remember." He opened his pocket watch and laid it on the desk. "Where was I?"

"The war."

"Yes. I never saw Stokes again, but I did run across him, in a manner of speaking."

"In the Army?"

"Yes, clever of you. I went into the Army's legal branch naturally. And there eventually I met someone who had defended Stokes at a court-martial. The charge was impersonating a brigadier, and wearing a chestful of medals to which he wasn't entitled. I wish I could remember the whole story, it was rather good. Evidently—" Portman hitched his chair closer, and began to look more than ever like a jolly butcher—"evidently, Stokes wanted to defend himself on the ground that he was in Military Intelligence—which he was, you know."

"I didn't know. He must have been important, then."

"Not really. He'd the nominal rank of major, but actually he wasn't fit for responsible duties. For some time, they'd had him working as a code clerk: deciphering simple items, and working alongside sergeants and lance-corporals. Then one day the Major started *inventing* messages himself. Complete rubbish. They put him on even lighter duties, but he got worse. Then he ran off without leave. They picked him up in Shropshire, I think it was, doing his impersonation. His defence was that God had sent him secret coded messages, elevating him in rank, and so on. He tried to put that forward at his court-martial.

"Naturally they found him not guilty, insane. He was hospitalized and finally given a medical discharge—or so I heard. That was about 1943."

"When I saw him," Phin said, "he was in dire poverty. Did you know that?"

"How could I? Haven't seen him since the club broke up. Oh, I see what you're driving at—what happened to his Army pension? Oddly enough, I think I do know something about that. It was a fine legal point my colleague was making, when he told me the story. Yes, I have it: the machinery was set in motion to strip the Major of his rank—to reduce him to a private—*before* he went crackers. So when he came out of the Army, that's what he was, a private. A pension that amounts to no more than a kick in the backside, in other words."

The intercom buzzed. "Five minutes, Mr Portman."

"Yes, all right. Well, Mr Phin, I think that must be all."

Phin shifted in his chair, but did not stand up. "Could you tell me a bit about the Seven Unravellers, then? And how Stokes fitted in?"

"Very well." With a sigh, Portman sat back. "The simple answer is, he didn't. He rather got on everyone's nerves. For one thing, he carried this little notebook about, and we all got the impression he was taking notes on *us*. We noticed, for example, that whenever anyone said something nice about the Russians, out came the notebook. Once, just showing off, I said that a good solicitor—such as I meant to be—could easily get a murderer acquitted, though guilty. I said that I hoped to do so one day, just to prove my point. Of course it was all pompous nonsense, but he put it down. That's the sort of thing I mean. He set everyone's teeth on edge.

"Beyond that, he didn't fit in much anyway. What the rest of us cared for was murder, not intrigues of espionage. Plain murder was after all the purpose of our little get-togethers. Though of course each of us had a different slant on it.

"There was Danby, our tame policeman. He liked American detective stuff, hard-boiled chaps dishing out sex and violence in equal measure. I suppose you're wondering what he thought of old Stokes? I think he hated him. It's hard to tell, Danby seemed to have a grudge against everyone. But he hated Stokes, I think, for being an officer and a gentleman. It may seem a trivial reason, but then Danby was a trivial person, always getting into little scrapes over imagined slights. *Machismo*, I believe, is the fashionable word for it now. Then it was just a chip on the shoulder."

"Anyone else who hated Stokes?"

"To most of us, he was just an irritating bore. But Hyde had reason enough to hate him. Gervase Hyde, the club aesthete. Spent most of his time lounging about, posing and trying to coin epigrams. Like something straight out the *The Yellow Book*, a relic from a vanished age. He was always talking about the so-called art of murder. By that, I think he meant really grisly crimes without any motive: bodies sawn up or dissolved in acid, brides in the bath, trunk murders. He kept on about the 'psychological angle', though I doubt he knew any more psychology than the rest of us. Real crimes seemed to interest him more than fictional ones. I think when he ran across an unsolved murder, he more than half hoped it would remain unsolved. But what was I saying?

"Oh yes, Hyde and Stokes. Bad blood from the start. Anything arty raised the Major's hackles, and anything vaguely homosexual did worse. Hyde was an arty poof, or he pretended to be, and Stokes could hardly stand being in the room with him. And if someone hates you that much, you're bound to reciprocate. More than one meeting ended with those two shouting 'Communist!' and 'Nazi!' at each other. The rest of us tried to pretend it was all good clean fun, but it was—war."

"And the others? How did they take Major Stokes?"

"Latimer was too steeped in his test tubes and retorts to take much notice of him, I'd say. And Sir Tony was too well-bred to be offended by anyone."

"Sir Anthony Fitch, is that?"

"Yes, my late father-in-law. He died in the blitz, anyway, so his opinion wouldn't matter now. And that leaves Dorothea. She's all right. Always treated Stokes like the child he really was. In fact she got along pretty well with everyone, in spite of . . . But I see our time's up."

"In spite of what?"

"Nothing, really. She was rather a cold bitch, but I expect age has mellowed her. Anyway, she certainly never was a murderess, and I think I've met enough to judge. Now our time *is* up."

The intercom buzzed twice. Phin got to his feet. "One more question. Does the name Green mean anything to you? Ever know anyone named Green connected with the Unravellers?"

"No. I know at least a dozen Greens, but none in the murder line. But aren't you going to ask me where I was at the time of the crime?"

Phin smiled. "I wouldn't dream of asking a solicitor for his alibi. Sorry to have taken up so much of your time, but I did feel it was urgent."

"I quite understand. I am pressed today, though. As it is, I'll have to vacate my office this afternoon while the glazier does my window. Some clever little vandal heaved an orange through it last night. Now there's a small mystery for you to chew on."

Phin appeared to think about it. "An orange? Let's see. Your office is near Drury Lane. Maybe the ghost of Nell Gwyn . . .?"

Portman laughed. He clapped Phin on the back, but also propelled him gently towards the door.

CHAPTER FIVE

PHIN HAD NEVER SEEN the Latimers' bungalow before, but he knew it well. He could have stopped outside, closed his eyes and drawn it from memory: the steep roof and double chimney, the round window by the front door, the pair of tall poplars rising in the background, set against a pile of sudsy cumulus. He even knew the black and white cat rolling in the grass.

As he remembered it, the scene required two more figures: a boy in cap and short trousers rolling a hoop; a girl with bobbed hair skipping. Underneath, the picture required three lines of heavy type: "Jack is playing. Jill is playing. Muff is playing too."

Shaking off his nostalgia, Phin stepped up the path (of crazy paving, of course—stop it, Phin!) and knocked.

A tall young woman answered. She had straw-coloured hair, freckles, and the kind of freshness that almost passes, in northern countries, for beauty.

"Mr Phin, is it? I'm Brenda Latimer. Come in—oops!" The black and white cat had made a run at the open door. With a practised gesture, the girl stopped it with a foot, scooped it up and flung it back on the lawn. "Come in quickly, before Maggie gets the idea again."

Brenda Latimer led him into a small parlour, where a weary-looking fat man in a pink shirt sat running his hands through his hair.

"Dad, this is Mr Thackeray Phin."

"Eh?"

"The *private eye.*"

47

He stood up to shake hands. "How do you do, Mr Phin. Dorothea phoned this morning to say you might be paying us a visit. She told me the dreadful news about old Stokes."

Leonard Latimer's plump jowls were covered with old acne scars, now almost invisible in the blandness of his face. Before taking Phin's hand he wiped his own on his drip-dry shirt, but his handshake was damp all the same. He seemed dazed. With the handshake over, he seemed unable to decide what to do with his hands, and finally put them behind him.

His daughter was cool and poised, by contrast. Her appearance suggested a secretary: unfrilly blouse and skirt in two shades of business-like blue; no jewellery; light make-up; pale hair worn neither sensually long nor faddishly short; and of course the hand she offered, with its short, plain-varnished nails.

The three of them stood there for an awkward moment, until Brenda said, "For goodness' sake, Dad, you've no manners at all! Please sit down, Mr Phin."

Latimer seemed to snap out of a trance. "Oh—sorry . . . yes, do sit down. The little woman's just making some coffee, if you'd like some?"

"Thank you." Phin sat down in a miniature armchair, and found the tiny coffee table jammed against his knees. Brenda folded herself into one corner of the sofa and opened a book. Her father took the other corner, and seemed to slip into his trance again.

"I'm sorry to barge in on you like this."

"No, no, it's all right. We're just—having coffee."

Brenda looked up from her book. "'You said that, Dad."

Phin cleared his throat. "The first thing I'd better ask is where you were the night before last, Mr Latimer. No offence, but I really thought I ought to ask everyone who knew Major Stokes."

"Dreadful business. Dorothea says it's murder." Latimer ran his hands through his thinning hair again. "Say, you don't think I did it? No, of course not. Night before last I was—where was I? Wednesday, was it? I was—"

"Dad, you were in Hamburg."

"Yes, of course. I'm losing track of time. Yes, the little woman

48

and I flew to Hamburg on Tuesday—Wednesday, I mean—and came back this morning."

"Fine. The next thing I'd like to ask is—"

Mr Latimer wasn't listening. Having begun speaking of Hamburg, he seemed unable to stop. "Terrible place. Couldn't get a wink of sleep in their so-called four-star hotel. That's one reason I'm so tired today—got my days and nights all turned about. Never can sleep anywhere but my own bed. Which is unfortunate, because I'll need to travel a lot, if I get this promotion. Sometimes I wish I'd stayed a simple research chemist, nine to five. I'm a bit old for these irregular hours. And the price of everything over there—terrible! I was glad to be back, I can tell you. We landed at Heathrow at half past six, and I wish we'd come back last night instead. Glad to be back. No, on second thoughts, I wasn't. We had the long drive home, and then our troubles were just beginning. What do you think we found?"

"Not that again," said Brenda.

"We found the house broken into, and Brenda asleep in her room, oblivious to it all. She could sleep through an air raid, that girl."

Phin nearly upset the tiny table. "A burglar? Last night?"

"She could sleep through an air raid," Latimer went on. "If they still had them, that is. They don't, so that hypothesis must go untested."

"What was taken?"

"Nothing. Not a whisker from the cat, nothing. Whoever it was slipped the lock on the back door, nipped in here, went through my desk, found nothing, and then messed up the place."

Phin looked over the room. "Seems all right now."

"Of course, I couldn't restrain the little woman from cleaning it up. She ran in to see if Brenda had been raped or murdered in her bed, then she rushed back in here and started in. Hadn't even taken her hat off. I tried to stop her."

"What exactly was this mess? Anything broken?"

"No, but furniture tipped over, cushions scattered about, ashtrays dumped. Magazines ripped up and scattered about, too."

"Did you call the police?"

"At once. I wondered about the 'Don't touch anything' rule, but decided the phone was safe enough, and anyway didn't feel much up to trotting down to the corner kiosk to dial the proverbial 999, you see?

"Well, by the time the boys in blue arrived, the little woman had very nearly put everything right. I don't think they half believed we'd had a burglary at all. I showed them the Yellow Pages, ripped asunder and scattered to the four winds, but that hardly convinced them, either. It wasn't until they saw the page stuck to the kitchen door that they sat up and took notice. One of the Yellow Pages. This one. Stuck to the door with a carving knife."

He fished in a waste-paper basket and passed Phin a page with a knife slit in the centre. The page was headed "Solicitors". Automatically, Phin looked for Portman's name, but the page ended with the Ds.

"Does this mean anything to you, Mr Latimer?"

"No. Say you don't think it's connected somehow with—with Stokes?"

"That's for you to say, really. What do you think the burglar was after?"

Latimer seemed to slip away again. "From time to time, I've kept a few company secrets in that desk," he murmured. "It could be that, or—I just don't know."

After a moment of silence, Phin asked, "Can you tell me anything about Major Stokes, then? When was the last time you saw him?"

"Let me see . . . Just after we went into the war. He reactivated his commission, and he turned up at our last meeting in uniform. We were all rather pleased he was going, glad to see the back of him. You see, he didn't get along. The club was supposed to be concerned with murder, but he could never quite keep on the subject. Always fiddling with codes and ciphers—kids' games like that. And spy stories. He read nothing else, and if you ask me, it affected his mind. There were times when I could talk to him for half an hour without finding out whether he was talking about fiction or reality. In the place we held our meetings,

Alberto's Restaurant, he used to think the Italian waiters were spies! I'm sure he even suspected us!"

"I understand he kept notes on some of the other Unravellers," Phin said.

"Yes, he—ah, here's the little woman. Vera, this is Mr Thackeray Phin."

Mrs Latimer, was in fact a little woman. She approached with an enormous tray of coffee and cakes and, though she seemed to be having no trouble with it, Brenda got up to take it from her. The little woman smiled in Phin's direction without looking at him directly. As soon as her hands were free, she whipped out a duster and attacked the mantel shelf.

"Carry on," she cried. "Don't let me disturb anyone."

Brenda said, "Mum, why don't you sit down with us?"

"Sit down? *Sit down?* I haven't the time, child. If I sat down, I hate to think what a state this house would get into."

"But what will Mr Phin think of us?"

"I don't know, I'm sure. I hope he won't think we're a family with nothing better to do than *sit down* all the time! Some of us have work to do, even if you and your father are 'too tired' to go to your jobs."

Brenda blushed. As she poured out coffee, she said, "Dad's got an excuse, at least, Mr Phin. His Hamburg trip really has taken it out of him. All I did was go out with Martin and some friends, and land myself with a hangover. That's why I didn't hear our prowler, of course. I'm afraid I was sleeping it off."

Phin sat back in the small chair and stirred his coffee. "Martin? I don't believe I know him."

"Oh, of course not, how silly of me. I just assumed that anyone who knew Aunt Dorothea would know her nephew Martin. My fiancé."

"We haven't met. Do you see much of Miss Pharaoh, then?"

"Lots. Martin's always over there, fixing up her old monstrosity of a house. So if I want to see him, I have to see quite a lot of her as well."

Latimer appeared to have slipped into his trance again. He held a cup of black coffee and stared into it. "I presume you've seen Miss Pharaoh off and on, then, over the years?" Phin asked him.

"Eh? Oh yes, off and on. How did you guess?"

"Your daughter's engaged to her nephew. That can't be a coincidence."

Latimer smiled. "Of course it's not, you're perfectly correct. Dorothea and I have kept in touch. She has a remarkably logical mind, for a—"

Brenda cut in: "Don't you dare say women aren't logical!"

It was Latimer's turn to blush. "Nicely intercepted, my dear. I ought to have said, Dorothea has a logical mind, fascinating in its deviousness and complexity. Have you seen any of her little logic problems, Mr Phin?"

"A few of them, yes. I agree, she's a genius. It's a pity with her intellect, that she never went in for an academic career. Since she had money, it would have been easy enough to have gone on and become a first-class logician—formally recognized, I mean."

"A professorship? Funny, I'd never thought of her that way. I suppose you're right, though. I suppose it must have been the War. Like most of us, she rather missed out on her youth. Didn't marry for the same reason, I expect."

Mrs Latimer took a framed photo from the mantel and handed it to Phin. "There's no mystery about that!" she said. "If you look at her when she was young, you can guess why she never married."

He looked at it: seven earnest faces, among whom he recognized the youthful Latimer and Portman and a pompous middle-aged man, just beginning to go bald, who could only be Major Stokes. The young Miss Pharaoh was not remarkably pretty, but otherwise he saw no hint of what Mrs Latimer evidently saw.

"I still don't understand," he said, handing the picture back.

Mrs Latimer wiped it clean of fingerprints and set it back in place. "She's wearing men's clothing," she said. "You can draw your own conclusions." Before he could ask more, she stalked off into the next room. Presently there came the whine of a vacuum cleaner.

Latimer looked as blank as Brenda. "Vera gets strange notions now and again," he said. "She's got some idea that Dorothea's a lesbian. Whenever Dorothea comes over, the little woman goes to bed with a headache or something—it's silly, but there you are. Dorothea's no more a lesbian than I'm King Farouk, but Vera won't drop the notion."

"Where did she get it?" Phin asked.

"The picture! The group photo! Just because Dorothea happened to be wearing that blasted man's suit—it was all a joke, really." Latimer poured more coffee. "You see, old Sir Tony got the notion he fancied Dorothea."

"That's Sir Anthony Fitch? The old man in the picture?"

"Yes. He really pestered her, the old goat, until it became embarrassing for all of us. Especially it embarrassed Dorothea. She told him to get lost in every possible polite way—and a few not so polite ways. At one meeting he offered to buy her a nice gown for a group photo. She declined. He insisted, saying that he wanted a picture of her to keep. That did it. I saw a light come into her eyes, and she agreed to buy 'something smart' for the photo session, charging it to Sir Tony. I had to give the old boy credit, he was able to laugh when he joke was on him."

"Have you explained this to your wife?"

"Oh, Vera never listens to anyone, especially me."

Brenda said, "Mum hasn't been too well, Mr Phin. She—"

"She'll have to see Dorothea at the wedding, anyway," said Latimer. "Maybe that'll put an end to her nonsense."

Phin said, "I understand Sir Anthony's dead now."

"That's right." Latimer sighed. "Only five of us left now. I expect I'll be next."

"Dad!"

"It's true. The old ticker's not what it used to be. Just like poor old Stokes—"

Phin interrupted. "You knew Stokes had a bad heart, then?"

"No. Though I'm not surprised. I was about to say, like poor old Stokes, I'm about to quit this mortal coil. It was his heart, was it?"

"We won't know until the inquest." Phin brought out a cheap spiral-bound notebook and opened it. "What I'd like to find out now is, who would have wanted Stokes dead?"

Latimer shrugged. "If you'll forgive me saying so, I think you're tackling this at the wrong end. Oughtn't you try to get *physical* evidence to start with? What have the forensic people come up with—the scene-of-the-crime boys?"

"I don't know, and I don't think the police are likely to tell me." Phin watched the black and white cat glide along a wall and stop to rub itself on a door frame. "I believe there was an interesting letter found, but the police aren't saying anything about it yet."

"Of course forensics have come a long way since my day," Latimer said. "It was never more than a hobby with me, but I still keep up my subscription to *The Criminologist* and one or two other journals. Do you know . . ." He launched into a lengthy account of a new technique, the gist of which seemed to be that if a man were found shot to death in an open field, it would be possible to tell which direction the bullet had come from, by nothing more than a detailed analysis of the soil around him.

Brenda suddenly addressed the cat. "Magwitch! What are you doing in here? If Mum catches you, she'll take about eight of your lives!" She dragged the animal from under a table and carried it to the front door. "Out!"

"Close the passage door," said Latimer. "He keeps coming in by his own private entrance. What's wrong, Mr Phin?"

"I was just thinking of Major Stokes's cat. He told Miss Pharaoh that some enemy had poisoned it. Maybe that's the kind of physical evidence we need, Mr Latimer."

Latimer rubbed his hair. "I don't see it. What's a cat got to do with evidence? Poisoning a cat isn't even a crime, is it?"

"No. In fact, if it's done humanely, it's not even a misdemeanour." Phin closed his notebook and got to his feet. "But it's all I've got to work with, isn't it?"

Old Hodge said nothing when he saw the stranger climbing over the wicket gate and picking his way down to the canal tow-path. Tall, skinny bloke it was, dressed like a foreigner and up to no good. Still, Old Hodge kept hisself to hisself and never said nothing to strangers. He didn't want trouble, but the good clasp knife in his pocket was always ready. He put his hand on it when the stranger spoke.

"Hello. Are you Old Hodge?"

"Might be. Who wants 'im?"

"My name is Thackeray Phin. They told me at the pub I might find you down here. At The Bargee."

"Find me? I ain't lost, Harry." Old Hodge picked up his boat hook and moved away down the path. There was something down there, all right. A glimmer of metal down in the green murky water. For the moment he forgot all about the stranger as he grappled with it. Bastard wasn't sinking, wasn't floating either, but it was heavy. Snagged on something, likely. He towed it in close and got a fist on it, and then the stranger was there beside him, getting his fancy sleeve wet. They hauled it up.

"Bleeding sewing machine!" An old treadle Singer, still in good condition. When he'd wiped the muck off and dried it, Old Hodge knew he'd get a couple of quid for it, no fear.

"What'll you take, Harry?" he asked the stranger. "Half a sheet see you all right?"

"What? Oh, I don't want any part of it. It's yours, Old Hodge. All I want is a little information."

"You ain't the Old Bill."

"You know I'm not. But I want to know something about the night before last. At the pub they told me you sleep down here sometimes, so I thought—"

Old Hodge laughed, showing two or three brown teeth. "The missus slippin' out on you, is she? Hee hee, not much of that on the tow-path any more. These days it's all motors they gets off in. But in the old days—"

"It's not that, exactly. I want to know if you saw anyone at all walking along here. Late. Someone on his own."

"Bloke, was it? On his tod? Three–four of them every night, I never pay no mind. Keep yourself to yourself, see?"

The stranger looked disappointed. "You wouldn't know any of them if you saw them again?"

"Naw, keep meself to meself. I been workin' this canal for forty year, pullin' out all the old rubbish they throws in. Seen a lot of

55

sights, but I never messes with anybody. I know more than I let on, more than I let on."

"Like what?"

"Like this sewin' machine. I know who threw it. It was Mrs Horrocks's son. I seen him haul it out in to her back garden yesterday, and her old copper, too. All just rubbish to 'im."

"Her copper?"

"You know, for boilin' clothes. Solid copper, that is. I expect he'll pitch that in, in a day or so, and it'll fetch me a penny, eh?"

The foreigner seemed to be thinking about something else. Finally he said, "Did you find anything unusual, yesterday or today?"

"Unusual like what?"

"That's just it, I don't know. But something you don't see every day. And that you don't know where it came from."

"Naw, naw. I knows every inch here, and what they pitch in. My livin', i'n' it?"

The stranger handed him a card. "If you do find anything, would you let me know? I'll pay a pound on top of whatever you'd get anywhere else. Anything really unusual. And I imagine you'll find it between the gate there and the middle of Tennyson Avenue. If it's there."

"If it's there, I'll find it, Harry."

Phin continued up the tow-path until he came to the rear of No. 44 Tennyson Avenue. Scrabbling up the embankment and climbing a rotten wooden fence brought him into the weed-choked back garden. There were pieces of iron junk rusting among the weeds, a possible treasure trove for Old Hodge.

He located the vent for the toilet, and found that he could barely reach a forearm through it. No one under six feet four would have that much luck, without standing on something. There were no ladder marks or any other impressions in the earth below the vent; only Phin's footprints.

"So much for that idea." Phine found a rusting shovel stuck upright in the earth and used it to smash in a kitchen window. He made a complete tour of the house, but the police had evidently cleared everything of interest. From the dank rooms with stained wallpaper, he could deduce nothing but poverty and a leaking roof.

One puzzling item was an empty china cabinet. It was cheap but well dusted, and the glass doors sparklingly clean.

"And nothing in it. What could he have kept—wait. Didn't I see something in the kitchen?"

The kitchen was dirty and full of lazy flies. Phin reached under the table and pulled out a cardboard box full of broken crockery.

"Clean edges, so recently broken. Let's see . . ." He sat on the grubby lino and began the painstaking work of the archaeologist. A shard showing part of a crest and the letters NG MAY T seemed to fit with another, HEY REI.

" 'Long may they reign'? A Coronation cup, I'll be bound. And here's another."

After an hour of jigsaw work, he recognized the crockery as a collection of thirty-odd Coronation cups and mugs, exactly what the Major would have kept in his china cabinet.

"Someone smashed it deliberately, that's for sure." He stood up, fought his way through the flies and out the back window. "Someone, and not kids. They'd have simply smashed the cabinet. Someone took every cup out and smashed it. Now, with luck, I'll find that cat."

The little grave was just where he'd expected it, by the back fence. To mark it there was a piece of shirt cardboard, threaded through with a red leather collar. He read the brass tag: BISCUIT.

With care, Phin scraped away soft earth until he reached the biscuit-coloured fur of a Siamese cat. Using the tip of the shovel, he lifted the corpse slightly to examine it.

It was then he discovered that the head was separated from the body.

It was five-thirty, and Linneas Laboratories were just about to lock their doors, when the wild American rushed in with something in a plastic bag.

"It's a rush job," he said. "I'll pay whatever it costs, but I need a report by tomorrow. Okay?"

"Well, I'll see . . . What is it exactly?" The man behind the counter looked at the bag apprehensively.

"Autopsy on a cat. I want poison tests, all the usual ones."

"A cat, you say? Well, I—"

"We have reason to believe the animal was killed in a cruel and unusual way. Chopped up alive. Unless you can prove a poison, we'll be taking legal action."

"We?"

"I represent the League for the Protection of Our Mammalian Friends," said the American, a wild gleam in his eye. "And I *demand* your co-operation."

"Demand? But surely, sir—"

"Otherwise—" the wild gleam focused on the counterman— "otherwise, we might begin to believe you're doing *animal experiments* in your lab, eh? Vivisection?"

The counterman wrote him a receipt for the bundle. And they say the *British* are crazy about pets, he thought.

Old Hodge had the idea as soon as the stranger left, more's the pity. It stood to reason if the sewing machine didn't sink, there was something underneath. He poled it up, sure enough:

"Unusual, he says! Hah! Well, this'll cost 'im a bob."

At five-thirty he went to The Bargee and tried phoning the number on the card. There was no reply.

"Who you callin', Old Hodge?" asked the publican. "New lady friend?"

Old Hodge slammed down the receiver. "You just pull me a pint of mild, Harry. And keep yourself to—"

CHAPTER SIX

NEXT MORNING, Phin managed to run Gervase Hyde to ground at the IPA, the Institute of Progressive Arts. This turned out to be a large, comfortable-looking Victorian building near Madame Tussaud's. From the outside, it seemed no more than another hospital or government office, except that its doors stood open and unguarded by any commissionaire. Instead there was a sign, warning of the current exhibitions:

STRUCTURED ENVIRONMENT
CONCEPTUAL UNITY
ANTI-TECHNOCRACY IN BULGARIAN DESIGN
ALBION ALTERNATIVISM

Phin strolled inside. The impression of hospital or office efficiency was even stronger: secretaries clattered along the corridors carrying sheafs of mimeographing, phones and typewriters sounded from distant offices, and a small group of dazed visitors stood in the centre of the lobby, studying an array of signs pointing off towards the different exhibitions. Phin followed the arrow for STRUCTURED ENVIRONMENT and entered a narrow tunnel swathed in silver PVC.

He emerged in the canteen, where a large number of persons sat sipping coffee, overlooked by gigantic photographs of dead film stars. Another arrow led him on into another corridor, which soon became a labyrinth of progress: along one passage the walls were clothed in stencilled T-shirts, a long and unvariegated collection which finally gave way to framed photos of, apparently, every stone in Scandinavia. He turned a corner and found himself in a gallery showing designs from a Bulgarian art school, chiefly designs for shopping bags. It was here that he remembered it wasn't STRUCTURED ENVIRONMENT he wanted at all, but CONCEPTUAL UNITY, and the door was just ahead of him, decorated with a mimeographed manifesto and a handful of feathers. He read:

> As a painter concerned with the movement across the interface of static structure and dynamic perceptor, my work has been concerned with inevitable progress through diverse multi-dimensional structure/situations, and exploration within the shape-shifting bio-energetic framework of expression. I now hope to bring together in a creative, non-exploitative dramatic context the collaborative efforts of people working in diverging areas of co-creativity. We are individuals, yet speak with one voice, in a radically new and expanding CONCEPTUAL UNITY.
>
> GERVASE HYDE

When Phin opened the door, the sound of a bassoon escaped. He looked in.

The room, as vast and deep as a television studio, was almost entirely in darkness. At first Phin could see little more than the spotlit bassoonist, sitting in a wheelbarrow in the middle of a raised stage. Then, as his eyes grew accustomed to the dark, he saw other figures:

A person with a giant shapeless head stood silhouetted at one corner of the stage, holding a scythe. Near-by stood a scaffold, with two more figures. Someone else lay encased in a black bag, writhing stage centre to the music of the bassoon.

More lights came on. The shapeless head was of papier mâché, with a clown face. On the scaffolding a girl was pretending to be caught in the bars, while a boy wearing a monkey mask pretended to menace her. Overhead another girl sat in a suspended crescent moon and—though it may not have been part of the show—picked her nose with great energy.

Suddenly Phin, too, was in the light. The monkey mask turned to regard him. "Just let it happen! You're part of it, too!"

"Well, really, I'm looking for Gervase Hyde. Is he here?"

The girl trapped in the scaffolding began to groan in improvisation: "Hyde. Looking. Hiding. Look. Looking for a place to hide, a face to hide in, to face Gervase in hiding."

"Come on, join us," said the monkey mask.

Phin saw no way out. He up-ended, walked a few steps on his hands, and then said, "I really am looking for him, though. It looks as though an old friend of his has been murdered. I'm a private detective."

"Great!" said the monkey mask. "Keep it up, man."

Feeling the strength in his arms failing, Phin lay down and pretended to take a nap through the rest of the performance. The others thanked him enthusiastically for his contribution, especially the nap. Finally, as they were about to troop off to the canteen, Hyde crawled out of his black bag and introduced himself.

"Thackeray Phin? Do I know that name?"

"I doubt it. Er—could I have a word with you in private?"

"Of course. The bar must be open by now. Follow me."

In the better light of the bar, Gervase Hyde turned out to be a plump man of sixty-odd, with shaggy grey locks and a drooping moustache. At a glance, he looked like anyone else at the IPA, only older. Yet his hair wasn't quite so shaggy, his expression not quite so solemn, and his denim suits showed signs of good tailoring. Without consulting Phin, he ordered two glasses of Pernod.

"Now, what's the mystery?"

"Miss Dorothea Pharaoh hasn't told you about me?"

"Ah! I knew I'd heard the name somewhere. So this is about the Unravellers, I take it. And poor Stokes."

"Yes. There are a few things about his death I'd like to clear up."

Hyde raised an eyebrow. "That sounds ominously like the words of Inspector Whatsit of the Yard. Why not just tell me of your theories, and I'll see what I can do."

"I don't have a theory. So far there's not much evidence of any kind. Do you have any theories?"

"Nice of you to ask, but no. On the one hand, Stokes was a most unpleasant man, who no doubt made plenty of enemies along the way. On the other hand, who'd bother? He was such a trivial person."

Phin looked at the Pernod, then shoved it across the table. "Here, you have it. Trivial? I suppose he was. No family. No money, and no real enemies that I can turn up. Until this re-union idea came up, I think he'd been utterly forgotten. No one seems to have seen him for years, of the Unravellers."

"Except me. Didn't Dorothea tell you? She got his address from me."

"I didn't know. And where did you get it?"

Hyde took a sip from the second glass of Pernod and sat back. "I ran into the Major a month ago, in Oxford Street. He was watching the buses go by and—I swear it—taking down their numbers. He didn't seem at all surprised to see me after all these years. Started in straightaway telling me about his 'work', as though resuming some old conversation.

"I was fascinated, of course, so I rather encouraged him. A bit of madness is always useful, to an artist. I bought him a cup of tea and pumped him. He gave me what I suppose is pretty much the whole story, the gist of it being that there was an international conspiracy afoot. The main objective was the invasion of Britain, no less, and he had all the details worked out. The arrangements of milk bottles on doorsteps, that was one kind of code, and the numbers of buses, that was another. He asked me: 'Why do you suppose that four No. 88 buses come along together?' I didn't know, I said, and he explained it was all part of the code.

"This went on for some time, and then he started on the Seven Unravellers. For me, at least, this was the interesting part. He said he'd taken the trouble to track all of us down. By his reckoning, at least one of us was a major cog in the international conspiracy machine. As he said, by finding out what we'd been up to all these years, he could fairly well tell who was what. And he said that one of us was behaving in a very suspicious manner. Frank Danby."

"I haven't met Mr Danby yet."

"Nor are you likely to meet him, if Stokes's story is in any way related to the truth. But it's a long story, and I need another drink? Are you sure you won't join me? Fruit juice?"

Phin finally accepted a glass of lukewarm rhubarb juice, and pretended to sip it while he listened.

"Danby was a policeman in the old days," Hyde said. "But somewhere along the line, he left the force. Stokes couldn't find out the reason—so of course he drew his own conclusions, or rather jumped to them. Danby then went to work for a small security firm, which over the years grew to be a large security firm. I believe he stopped delivering payrolls and took up some minor desk job. Then a couple of years ago—or anyway sometime before I met Stokes—he retired. He went to a village on the south coast, and became a total recluse. Stokes managed to run him to earth there.

"Not suspicious in itself, you may think, but of course we must see this through Stokes's eyes. He convinced himself that Danby was there for a purpose, perhaps to send signals to enemy submarines lying offshore or something equally sinister. So he paid him a visit. No one locally seemed to know a thing about him, but Stokes finally managed to find his cottage. Danby ordered him off the place. Threatened to set his dog on him."

Phin said, "Yes, but what had Stokes said to him? Did he go down there making wild accusations?"

"He said not. The minute Danby heard who he was, he turned violent. Mind you, Danby always was a violent bastard, but mainly when drunk. But the Major said that Danby was specially nasty this time. He said that if he ever caught Stokes near his house again, *he'd kill him.*"

Phin's hand shook, spilling the rhubarb juice.

"I thought that would interest you, Mr Phin. A threat like that. It interested me, too. I asked Stokes what he thought was the answer. Of course that only started him off again on the invasion conspiracy. I stood it as long as I could, and finally said goodbye. But I did exchange addresses with Stokes, and I took care to get Danby's address, too."

"So you were that much interested?"

"Oh, yes. You see, I used to amuse myself at the Unravellers by imagining how each of us would go about a murder. What type of strange psychological quirk might set one of us off, I wondered. And how would he go about it? Some of the members such as old Sir Tony Fitch, never made the grade. I simply couldn't imagine the old fellow killing anyone under any circumstances.

"But Frank Danby was just the opposite. It was all too easy to imagine him a hammer killer, say, moved by sudden rage over the most trivial incident. And his living by the sea like that made me think of it again. How easy, once you've beaten someone's head to jelly, to take the body out to sea and dump it overboard. And then, if you're the kind of person I think Danby is, you might take a special satisfaction in sitting in your house, looking out at the sea—knowing that it holds your secret."

"Did you pay him a visit?"

"No." Hyde laughed. "Actually I haven't the courage for real sleuthing. I thought about it, but the more I thought, the sillier it all seemed. If on the one hand the man's merely retired and likes his privacy, I'd feel a fool. If on the other hand he's a homicidal maniac, I wouldn't feel much like facing him. So I put it off indefinitely."

"Did you ever visit Stokes, then?"

"No, I'm not that fascinated with paranoia. One dose was enough."

Phin brought out his notebook and turned over the pages. "I don't seem to be getting very far with this," he said. "Do you have a pet of any kind?"

"No. Why do you ask? Do I look like a pet owner?"

"It's only your mentioning Danby's dog. I noticed that Leonard Latimer and Dorothea Pharaoh both have cats, and Major Stokes had a cat, but it—"

"Are you trying to tie this to the Unravellers somehow?"

Phin turned a page. "It's possible. Have you had any burglars or prowlers lately? I see that—"

"How very odd." Hyde set down his drink and put his elbows on the table. "Do you know, I may have had a prowler last night!"

"May have had?"

"All I know is, when I got up this morning, my front door was standing wide open. I'd had some people over in the evening, and my first thought was that one of them had somehow left it open. Then I remembered, I'd seen them out myself. I know that door was shut when I went to bed."

"What sort of lock is it?"

"Oh, a plain latch. Anyone could open it with a credit card—I've done it myself when I've forgotten my key. Anyway, my next thought was to see what had been taken. So I went over the place pretty thoroughly. The only things of value are a few paintings—other people's, alas—and a little Giacometti I managed to pick up in . . . But of course you're not interested in that. Needless to say, the only reason I'm a sane man today is that nothing was touched. The burglar took nothing! Perhaps he was awed by my good taste?"

"Nothing was moved or disarranged?"

"No, but in fact the burglar left me a little note. Here." Hyde unbuttoned his pocket and fished out a filing card. "It's gibberish to me, though it looks like some sort of chemical formula. Look."

Phin took the card by the edges and examined it. One side was blank, and the other bore this diagram:

$$\text{CO} \quad \text{OC}$$
$$\text{C}\!=\!\text{C}$$
$$\text{NH} \qquad \text{HN}$$

"Done with an ordinary-looking ballpoint pen," Phin said. "And I'm afraid it's an ordinary 3 x 5 file card. I suppose that also means no fingerprints." He sighed.

"Fingerprints? Lord, I hadn't thought. I've shown it to dozens of people here at the IPA this morning." Hyde took back the card and put it away. "But what does it mean? That's the question."

Phin couldn't resist the opening. Putting on a serious face, he said, "Ah, what does anything mean? Or to put it in aesthetic terms, it doesn't mean, it just *is*."

"Very funny. But isn't it a chemical formula?"

"I think so. If it were, what would that mean to you?"

65

Hyde thought for a moment. "Well. Let me play detective for the moment. You asked if I had pets, because other Unravellers had them. Then you asked if I'd had a prowler. So other Unravellers must be having them—right?"

"Right."

"Well then, what about Leonard Latimer? He's some sort of chemist at a soap company. Could he have left this?"

Phin nodded. "Meaning what, though? A warning? A reminder?"

"I simply can't imagine." Hyde's wry smile vanished for a moment, and he looked worried. "You don't suppose Latimer did for old Stokes?"

Phin finished making notes. "I don't know what to suppose," he said. "But I get the impression that some of the Unravellers, or maybe all of you, are holding out on me. One of you at least must know something important. That or else . . ." He paused for a long moment, staring at the closed notebook. Then he looked up. "Or else it's a joke."

"What?"

"A joke, and in the worst possible taste. Seizing upon the occasion of Major Stokes's death to manufacture a little mystery for the club."

Hyde laughed. "Well, don't look at me! I've never played a so-called practical joke in my life. Nor have any of the others, except the late Sir Tony."

Abruptly he stopped laughing, and his eyes widened. "Say, there's mystery and enough for you! There was something fishy about Sir Tony's death, too."

"Fishy how?"

"Something about the identification of the body. He was bombed in the blitz or something, and I suppose they had trouble identifying a lot of victims. But—I may be wrong now—the papers said they had the wrong body. He wasn't dead after all. Yes, I'm sure that was it. He wasn't dead at all."

"That suggests a couple of possibilities," said Phin. "What if he were alive still, and seeking revenge?"

"Oh, I like that. That's good. Except that he wouldn't want

revenge on anyone I can think of except Portman, for marrying his daughter after all. And except that Sir Tony would now be something like ninety years old! Not the age for antics."

Phin thought for some reason of Old Hodge, surely a nonagenarian and still able to manhandle heavy objects out of the canal. But:

"Yes, you're right. A silly notion. Suppose, instead, Sir Tony were the first victim, and Stokes the second? After all, these little 'clues' everyone seems to be getting must have some meaning."

"I like that, too." Hyde wiped his moustache. "Someone means to wipe us all out, like the Ten Little Persons of African Descent. You an Agatha Christie fan?"

"Who," said Phin, "is Agatha Christie?"

"Flowers, Miss Pharaoh?" Phin shifted the phone to his other ear. "When did this happen?"

"Last night. And only one variety was taken. It's very puzzling."

"Sounds like kids." But that, Phin thought, was what they kept saying about Stokes's minor disasters.

"Martin said it might be a kids' prank, too. But we've found a large, well-defined *adult* footprint in the soft earth. Not Martin's or Sheila's or mine, so whose?"

"Well, you could—"

"We are. Martin's mixing the plaster of Paris just now. No one can steal flowers from my garden and get away with it."

"You know, this may be one of a series of incidents." Phin told her briefly what had happened to the other Unravellers: Portman's vandal, Latimer's burglar, Hyde's burglar.

"And Major Stokes's burglar?"

"He's real, all right. Deliberately smashed his collection of Coronation cups—took them out of the cabinet to break them. As for his pet cat . . ."

"Some other time, Mr Phin, I must go. Plaster of Paris simply won't wait. Even if it is an anagram of 'Flip Sara presto'. Goodbye."

Phin hung up and rushed out to the Linneas Laboratories. As soon as he'd left, the phone began to ring.

CHAPTER SEVEN

CHIEF INSPECTOR GAYLORD did not look up from his desk. "Have a chair, Phin. Come to waste more police time, have you?" He opened a folder and began to read, making tick marks. Phin sat down and did not reply until he'd finished.

"I don't think I'm wasting police time, not any more. You see, the Unravellers have begun to suffer a—a plague of mysteries."

Gaylord looked at him. The American was wearing a fawn suit, yellow kid gloves, spats over patent-leather shoes. The shoes, like his full cravat and the homburg and walking stick he carried, were of a deep, purple-tinged brown.

"Phin, there's only one thing you can tell me," he said. "Who the hell's your haberdasher?"

"Like the clothes, do you?"

"No, I want to arrest the bastard, for fraud. God, you look like best man at a pimp's wedding."

Phin shrugged. "Whenever you've finished the tough-cop banter, I have something to tell you. As we say down at the brothel, I have information to lay."

"Wait, we can save a lot of time if I tell you something first." Gaylord closed the folder and opened another. "I have the post-mortem report on Edgar Stokes. He died of natural causes: a heart attack. Death probably took place between ten p.m. and two a.m. I have to ask you if you saw anyone enter the house during that time."

"I didn't."

"Not that it matters anyway. There you have it. The old man went to the toilet, suffered a heart attack, couldn't get back upstairs to his medicine, and died. That's pretty much how we read it."

"Okay, how about his fingernails?"

"All of the blood under them was his own. It looks as though he clawed about, broke his nails and bled from the quick."

"And paint?"

Gaylord cleared his throat. "Uh, no paint under his nails."

"None at all?"

"No. Phin, I don't see that that's specially relevant, in view of everything else. Do you want to make a case out of that?"

The sleuth drew off one of his gloves and lit a cigarette. "Inspector, it's a little like Holmes's dog that didn't bark, isn't it? I mean, the little room was completely covered with dry, flaky paint. Apparently the old man knocked a lot of it off in his death throes. And yet not a particle of it turns up under his nails. I believe the obvious question is: Who or what was he clawing at?"

"The toilet itself, perhaps." Gaylord turned a few pages of the file. "No, there's no blood on it. But look, Phin, these things happen. I've got hundreds of peculiar cases where things don't *quite* explain themselves. Most of them mean nothing at all."

"I'm still wondering about that letter."

"Then wonder no longer." Gaylord fished a thick manila envelope from his bottom drawer and passed it over. "The Ministry of Defence lads sent this back to us today, with a rude note. Give us a receipt and it's yours. Only promise not to bring it back again, eh?"

"Thank you. But of course you'll want it back. For evidence at the murder trial."

"I very much doubt that, Phin. I really do doubt it. What else did you have to tell me, besides nothing?"

"I found a decapitated cat in his back garden."

"*Another* murder? Any clues? Signs of a struggle? Or maybe the animal quarrelled with another cat in public?" Gaylord's sarcasm was true to its name, for his teeth were actually beginning to show. "Perhaps the cat was about to change its will, cutting out a certain kitten?"

"When you're through." Phin waited. "As a matter of fact, I had the cat tested for poison. There wasn't a trace of it."

"Who said there was? Phin, sometimes I think you're—"

69

"Miss Pharaoh said there was. She supposedly had it straight from the Major."

"So she misheard him. Ask her, not me. I only try to work here."

"I also took the trouble of examining the Major's broken crockery—that box in his kitchen. It was, until recently, a collection of Coronation cups."

"So he killed his cat and smashed his cups. Or someone did."

"Someone, but not the Major. Inspector, no one murders his pet and then buries it, marking the grave. No one smashes his hobby collection, then gathers up every single piece of it and keeps it. In every way, the Major behaved exactly like what he said he was—the victim of a vicious persecution."

"Back to Mr Green, are we?"

"And back to the Seven Unravellers, I'm afraid. Listen to this." Phin flipped open his spiral-bound notebook and read aloud:

"Tuesday night, Stokes dies, after complaining that he's been persecuted by someone named *Green*. Wednesday night, someone heaves a piece of fruit through the window of Portman, the solicitor, one of his fellow Unravellers. It's an *orange*. The same night, a prowler messes up Latimer's home, tears a sheet out of the *Yellow* Pages, and sticks it to a door with a knife."

"Sounds like a practical joker."

"So I thought. But there's more. Last night, a prowler enters Hyde's house—he's the artist—and leaves a calling card. A file card, that is, with a chemical formula written on it. This afternoon, after I visited the cemetery, I checked up on this in a library. It's a simple formula, in all the organic chemistry books —the formula for *indigo*."

"By God!" Gaylord mugged feigned astonishment. "Phin, I do believe you're on to—nothing. Is there more?"

"Yes. Inspector, would you be so good as to telephone Miss Dorothea Pharaoh now, and ask about the little theft she suffered last night?"

"Really, is all this necessary? Just tell me, without all the dramatics."

"I'd like to tell you, but I swear I don't know. I've made a guess, and I want you to help confirm it."

Gaylord dialled, asked a question, and groaned at the answer. "You were right," he said, putting down the phone. "Her flower thief took nothing but *violets*. Now, did you mention a cemetery? Let's have all of it."

"I made some enquiries and learned that another member of the club, Sir Anthony Fitch, is buried in Kensal Green Cemetery."

"Am I supposed to say 'Aha! Kensal *Green*'?"

"Wait for it. I went out there, and I must have just missed our busy prowler. Or should I say vandal? He'd just done a job of defacement on the tombstone of Sir Anthony Fitch. Daubed a big question mark on it, in acrylic paint. *Cerulean blue*."

"You seem very certain about the exact colour and type."

"Oh, he left the tube. I merely read what it said. See?" Phin drew a plastic bag from his pocket and held it up to show the squashed tube of paint. Then he dropped it on the desk.

"I don't suppose there'll be prints, but there it is. And as I say, I must have just missed the person who did it. Because I'm told acrylic dries within minutes." Phin drew off his remaining glove and held up one blue-tipped finger. "And that's my case so far."

Gaylord bent his aquiline nose over the tube of paint, as though about to attack and devour it. "I do a bit of Sunday painting myself, you know. This is not a popular brand. I expect we could trace it."

"I have a feeling you'll find it came from the house of Gervase Hyde," said Phin. "It would fit the pattern. Like the chemical formula, pointing suspicion at Leonard Latimer, the research chemist. And at Latimer's house, the torn-out Yellow Page listed only solicitors. I wouldn't be surprised to find out that Sir Anthony Fitch was an importer of oranges, or fond of violets or—God knows, an Irish patriot."

The policeman looked at his watch. "Anything else? I'm willing to help you with your little charade, but I really can't spare the time to sit and listen. All you've shown me so far is that some practical joker is laying clues about with a trowel. Burglaries?

71

Colours? What do they all add up to? o + o + o = o. You might as well try mixing all the colours together on a palette, to get a big blob of grey muck—a big grey nothing. All I know is, Stokes is dead, we think he died naturally, and there's an end to it. Now, Phin, I want you to take yourself out of here. As a favour to me, don't come back. Oh, and don't forget your all-important letter, eh?"

Seeing the great length of the letter, Phin took his phone off the hook and settled down to read it undisturbed. It was addressed to "The Director, M.I.6", and marked "MOST SECRET AND URGENT".

Dear Sir,

When I first began my study of the Communist conspiracy nearly forty years ago, I had no idea of its size, of the reach of its insidious tentacles. I began by merely keeping a few odd notes on possible Russian espionage in Britain. They were haphazard notes, kept on a day-to-day basis, and I have since destroyed them as valueless.

As time went on, it became increasingly clear that this espionage and subversion effort was highly successful. Russia was in fact waging and winning a secret war within the very shores of our sceptred isle.

It must be obvious that at the end of the Second World War, Britain was an empire and a world power. Yet we gave away this power with both hands. Stalin's minions were given the greater part of Europe. India left the empire, followed by a host of lesser colonies. Spies sold our atomic secrets, while here an army of "spontaneous" demonstrators protested at Britain's having an atom bomb of her own! Finally the process culminated with two disasters: Russia launched her first space satellite, and Britons began to acquire a taste for *vodka*.

I realize that in these days of vodka-swilling and package tours to Leningrad, it has become unfashionable to see Russia as a danger. This too is part of the plan. Yet I have proof positive of an imminent invasion, coming within five years!

That is when the robot-like workers of France (most of them Communists) will have finished digging *their* tunnel under *our* Channel.

My training in cryptanalysis has been invaluable in discovering the master plan of this invasion. Knowing that the infamous drink *vodka* was being used to dull the liberty-loving brains of British subjects (I notice that a vodka drinker never looks you in the eye), I examined the name itself. *Vodka* has five letters, concealing a key to the insidious Five-Year Plan. If one writes *vodka*, then moves down five letters in the alphabet, another word appears.

$$\underline{\text{V}} \quad \underline{\text{O}} \quad \text{D} \quad \text{K} \quad \underline{\text{A}}$$
$$\text{w} \quad \text{p} \quad \text{e} \quad \text{l} \quad \text{b}$$
$$\text{x} \quad \text{q} \quad \text{f} \quad \text{m} \quad \text{c}$$
$$\text{y} \quad \text{r} \quad \text{g} \quad \text{n} \quad \text{d}$$
$$\underline{\text{Z}} \quad \underline{\text{S}} \quad \text{H} \quad \underline{\text{O}} \quad \underline{\text{E}}$$

The meaning of *z-shoe* is obvious: "For want of a nail, the *shoe* was lost; for want of a shoe, the horse was lost; for want of a horse, the *battle* was lost." I assumed this innocent-sounding saying concealed the entire battle plan, in three main phases. The "nail" phase was already past; we were now in the middle of the "shoe" (vodka) phase.

The coming phase would, I knew, involve horses. I studied references to horse-racing for a clue, not without success. Many of the names of race winners appeared to be veiled references to *Russia*, or to *Reds*. Could it be only coincidence that horses such as *Nijinsky* (a Russian dancer), *Russian Hero* and *Red Alligator* were listed as winning? Or did I detect the subtle hand of the NKVD secret police? I think your office must investigate this: it may be that race-horse owners are being influenced (either by vodka drinking or by a type of hypnotic ray from space) in their choice of names.

The full confirmation of this came with the winner of the

Grand National in 1973: a horse named *Red Rum*. Rum=
vodka, horse=shoe, and the series is complete!

However, my activities have not gone undiscovered. Somehow (possibly through satellite surveillance) the Reds have found
me out. In the reading room of my local library I might look up
to see some stranger staring at me—or else deliberately looking
away from me! In the supermarket, I heard strangers discussing
me out of sight in the next aisle. It became impossible to avoid
being shadowed in the street: if I turn a corner to avoid one
agent, another quickly takes up the trail. When I go to the
laundrette, women agents posing as ordinary housewives sit
watching my reflection in the glass doors of the washing
machines.

Now I know they mean to kill me. My first intimation of this
was the theft of milk off my doorstep: a pathetic attempt to
force me to drink the poison from Russia instead. Also the doorbell was rung at odd hours, a method familiar to Pavlov and
other Russian scientists, intended to make me thirst for vodka.

When these early operations failed, a man named Green (not
his real name, obviously!!) came to call. He tried to bribe me
to go away for a "nice holiday" (from which I should never
return!) and then he began to bully and threaten. I could be put
away in a mental hospital, he said. I could have an "accident",
being an old man on my own.

My resistance must have astonished him. His type expect
little resistance from those of advanced years and apparent
frailty, for they are of the breed of filthy rat whose courage
shows only against the weak. He growled a final threat and slunk
off into the night. In the morning, I found Biscuit, my cat
brutally murdered in the back garden.

I buried Biscuit, and informed the police. They of course
dismiss it all as the work of neighbourhood children. This may
be so, for the Reds are not above employing innocent babes in
their filthy work.

I know now that I am scheduled for "liquidation". I am all
the more certain since I discovered that *Red Rum* is simply
murder spelt backwards. I am resigned to death, but I refuse to

die in silence. Therefore I am writing to you of the invasion plan, hoping that my warning comes not too late . . .

From here, the letter ran to even greater extravagances, and to another 46 pages of the same cramped script. The Major spoke casually of thought-control devices and death rays, of a plan to poison British sweets, and of a plan to bore through the earth's crust beneath Britain and turn the island into a "volcanic holocaust". The most complex and far-reaching plans were deduced from the most banal material: a close observation of the number plates on parked cars gave the timetable for Armageddon; the innocuous clues of crossword puzzles gave him the names of "all top-ranking agents of the NKVD". It was all beautifully lucid and logically sound, and of course hopelessly mad.

Phin read it through, half-horrified at the writer's obvious mental anguish, half admiring his fertile imagination. The letter stopped just short of Martians and the Great Pyramid, but it was of the same order of madness: An unhappy, lonely, probably ailing old man magnifying his misery into a world-wide plot against him.

In a sense, the plot was all too real. The world had indeed turned against old people like Major Stokes. The battle was not between the long-defunct "NKVD" and "M.I.6"—it was between that sinister and nebulous force called Modern Society and a handful of forgotten pensioners. Society, employing the weapons of neglect, starvation, indifference and bureaucracy, was certain to triumph.

Where the mysterious Green fitted in, Phin could only guess: a welfare worker, a rent collector, or perhaps only a well-meaning but interfering neighbour. He had perhaps offered the Major help, but too late—the Major now saw every caller as an enemy, every helping hand as a threatening fist.

Phin sat back and rubbed his eyes. Somehow the sun had gone down and the evening slipped on without his noticing. On his way to the kitchen to make a pot of strong coffee, he stopped to draw the curtains.

A night mist had come over London, and the sodium-vapour street lamps made it glow yellow-orange. It was nothing to compare with the great pea-soupers of the past, those oppressive, lethal fogs that made London history. All the same, it held a promise of evil. Phin thought of Holmes and Watson in a four-wheeler hurrying through the invisible streets to prevent a murder. He thought of Prufrock, hurrying through the yellow fog to an appointment with cold, murderous lust. And he thought of Graham Greene's shabby, hunted confidential agent, fleeing from those who "would probably try to take advantage of the fog".

How easy it would be at this moment to slip quietly into the Major's madness, to imagine some Conspiracy out there in the mist: plotters spinning out the filaments of a gigantic web, drawing in their victims one by one . . .

He drew the curtains and picked up the receiver on his phone. "There is no plot," he said, waiting for Miss Pharaoh to answer. "There's nothing but a mad major and a dead cat and a box of broken crockery. There's nothing else at all, Gaylord's right. o + o + o = o. Hello, Miss Pharaoh?"

"Mr Phin! What a coincidence, I was just about to phone you. You see, I'm planning a little seaside excursion, and—"

"Yes, but first let me ask you this: Are any of the Unravellers interested in meteorology?"

"Sorry? I thought you said meteorology."

"I did. Any amateur weathermen in the group?"

"I have no idea. Why do you ask?"

"No reason. It's just that meteorologists sometimes use balloons."

Miss Pharaoh, after a slight hesitation, began talking about her excursion. It was clear from her tone that she felt the seaside air would do him no harm at all.

CHAPTER EIGHT

A LINE OF CARS was drawn up at the kerb before Miss Pharaoh's great house. Miss Pharaoh, holding her enormous fuchsia-coloured garden hat in place with one hand, flitted along the line, leaning down to talk to each car's occupants.

"I'll give her that," said Brenda. "She looks colourful, at least. But that dress with the flaming red poppies! Where did she dig it up?"

Martin nudged her. "She's quite proud of it," he said. "Don't say a word."

Miss Pharaoh checked everything: Did they understand the route? Was everyone here? Wasn't it best if everyone followed Martin, who had a map? Had Sheila fetched the hamper? Who was missing? Mr Phin?

Alone in his silver-grey Rolls at the head of the line, Derek Portman gripped the wheel, looked at his watch, gripped the wheel again. Ten past nine. A quarter past.

In the next car, Miss Pharaoh's gleaming yellow mini, Mia Tavener began to whine. "Shh, don't be cross," Sheila whispered. "We'll be off in a minute." She rather admired Miss Pharaoh's dress—they said all that nineteen-forties gear was coming back—and wished she had something herself to wear that wasn't like her work clothes: smock and tatty jeans.

Next was Leonard Latimer's sensible and elderly Rover, in which he and Gervase Hyde had just run through five minutes of small talk and discovered they had nothing further to say to one another. It was going to be a long drive.

"Hot," said Latimer. His hand played a game of church-and-steeple on the steering wheel. "But looks like rain."

Miss Pharaoh flitted along to the last car, where Martin and Brenda were giggling over some private joke.

"Are we all ready, then?"

Martin nudged Brenda. "Didn't I tell you? Yes, Aunt Dorothea, *we*'re ready. The hamper's in the boot, the car is ready, and we're all ready. Hop in."

She put her hand on the door handle but paused. "I do wish Mr Phin had shown himself."

Martin said, "He's probably overslept. You might as well—"

"Here he is."

A taxi turned the corner and drew up. Phin stepped out, and Brenda suppressed a scream of laughter.

The American detective was wearing white trousers and shoes, a crested blazer, and a boater. A string ran from the brim of his boater to his lapel, where it was fastened beneath an enormous white carnation. He paid the taxi driver and strode towards them, making a lunge with his green umbrella at every stride.

"Sorry I'm late," he said. "I stopped off to make a photocopy of Major Stokes's letter. For you, Miss Pharaoh."

"Mr Thackeray Phin, I'd like you to meet my nephew Martin Hughes, and his fiancée—"

"Not officially yet," said Martin. Brenda giggled.

"His fiancée, I repeat, Brenda Latimer."

"We've met. Hello again, Miss Latimer. You look ready for some sun."

"So you're the private eye," said Martin. "I suppose you can tell me all about myself just from my appearance?"

Phin looked at him, as they shook hands. "Well, you're not a Freemason or an asthmatic, how's that for a start? I mean you didn't offer me a secret handshake, and you don't wheeze."

"Thanks." When they'd laughed, Phin went on: "You attended a good school, but not a public school—Addlington Grammar? Yes? You work a bit with your hands, but not daily. And you're pretty careful with money."

Brenda gasped, and Martin burst out laughing again. "You are good! I see the work bit—you noticed my light calluses. But how did you guess my school? The accent?"

78

"No, but when I visited your aunt I saw a photo of you in your school uniform."

"Aha! And she told you I'm mean with money?"

"No. But she mentioned that you were a successful builder, yet your car isn't specially grand, nor are your clothes. And the little cuts on your chin tell me you like to get every bit of good out of a razor blade."

Martin roared with laughter, and Miss Pharaoh's gold tooth winked. Only Brenda seemed embarrassed.

"Get in," said Miss Pharaoh. "You can ride with us."

Phin looked over the line of cars. "Uh, I thought I'd have a word with Mr Portman."

"Nonsense. I want to hear how you're progressing with this case. Get in."

Finally they were off. Martin's car moved out slowly, and the others fell in behind. Brenda rolled down her window and lifted her hair, feeling the breeze. "Might be nice enough for a swim," she said. "If the sun comes out."

The two detectives in the back seat ignored the hint; they were poring over the Major's letter.

"As I expected," said Miss Pharaoh at length. "Mad as a hatter's tea party."

Phin nodded. "But still murdered?"

"I think so. We may find out more today." She leaned forward and tapped Martin on the shoulder. "My dear, you're sure you brought the hamper?"

"Aunt Dorothea, for the last time, I hope, I myself carried the hamper out and put it in the boot. Now put it out of your mind and enjoy yourself."

"Now that you mention it, I *do* enjoy myself. Immensely. I enjoy being healthy and reasonably sane." She tapped the letter. "And I enjoy being the same size in clothes as I was when I was twenty. What do you think of the frock, Brenda?"

Brenda turned to look. "I—er—"

The gold tooth gleamed again. "Not fair of me to ask, was it? It's not exactly *fetching*—or whatever they say these days—but I'm really too old to give a damn. I like your outfit, though."

Brenda smiled her thanks. She wore a simple yellow sleeve-less dress, with a matching band in her neat hair. Phin knew without looking that there would be a matching handbag and shoes, and that in the handbag there would be a pair of large sunglasses which Brenda would wear pushed up on the top of her head.

Miss Pharaoh went back to the letter, while Phin watched the suburbs roll past. In a moment there came from the front seat the sound of a handbag snapping closed. Brenda brought out a pair of over-sized sunglasses, tucked the bows into her hair and pushed the lenses up on top of her head.

"Martin," said Miss Pharaoh, "are you sure we're on the right road?"

"I've been over the AA map again and again, Aunt Dorothea. While we were waiting for you. Anyway, I never get lost."

Brenda giggled. "Never? What about our camping trip in France, darling?" She grinned at those in the back seat. "We were supposed to join a group and go boating down the Loire last month. But did we?"

Martin's neck blushed. "But that was a simple—"

"Lost on the river, were you?" Phin asked.

"We never got *to* the river," Brenda explained. "At the ap-pointed hour, we were miles away, driving round in circles in— was it Limoges? Missed the others entirely, and had to put up at some dreadful little hotel . . ."

Martin nudged her, and she added, "Separate rooms, of course."

Dorothea Pharaoh snorted. "I hope I'm neither so naïve as to believe that, nor so old as to be shocked by the truth. Besides, I know that no power on earth could persuade Martin to pay out for *two* rooms."

The blush spread to Martin's ears, but he said nothing.

"Unfair," said Brenda. "We had a marvellous time and Martin didn't complain once. Even though we'd paid for the group trip *and* for the dinghy which we never even unpacked and got wet. Still, there's always next summer. We can get lost near some other river."

Martin groaned. "All right, I'm a dreadful driver and a

Scrooge. But I'm sure Mr Phin would rather talk about murder."

"There's not much to talk about," Phin said. "I'm willing to go along with you, Miss Pharaoh, in believing that someone killed the Major. Trouble is, that's as far as I can take it. I don't know how he was killed. I don't know why. I don't know by whom. And right now, I don't know if any of it will ever make sense. How about you?"

Miss Pharaoh shrugged. "I have a hypothesis or two, but there's really no point in going into them, until I find some proof." She tapped the letter. "And this is anything but proof—most discouraging."

"What's in it?" Brenda asked.

"The Major's explanation of the end of the world," said Miss Pharaoh. "The Russian takeover of Britain, which evidently begins with his death."

Martin looked round. "You don't suppose—?"

"No, I don't, and keep your eyes on the road, young man. I don't intend that we should all join Major Stokes in his happy cipher room in the sky, not just yet."

"Cipher room?" Brenda looked blank. "Is it in code or something?"

"Oh yes, in a private code, accessible only to the Major and six-year-old children," Miss Pharaoh flipped through the pages. "I always knew Stokes was a fool."

Martin cleared his throat. "Aunt Dorothea! The man is dead."

"Yes, yes, but his foolishness lives on, doesn't it? If he could have forgotten about his blessed Red conspiracy for one second and come down to earth, he might at least have told us something useful. Suppose this Green person killed him? He could have described him, and we'd have somewhere to start. But no . . ."

Phin said, "At the same time, you'll have to admit he was ingenious at times. I thought the '*Red Rum* equals *murder*' idea was admirable. A horse of another colour."

"I suppose so," she grumbled. "A horse of another colour, if you like. A race-horse of another race. *Now recap: pacer won.*"

Phin was the first to appreciate the palindrome. "I see what

81

you mean: word play is as easy as horseplay, and about as meaningful."

The wind began to flap Miss Pharaoh's hat. She drew out the long pins and removed it. "Exactly. The Major's logic may be sound enough, but he argues from a wrong premiss: the preposterous notion that there is a world-wide Red conspiracy against him. If we grant the Major's premiss, we grant all the absurdities that follow. Anything red becomes suspect, and anything not-red becomes equally suspect, eh? *Green*, he says, is a synonym for *red*! He might just as well say that—that a robin redbreast is the same bird as a blue tit!"

"Aunt Dorothea!" Martin blushed again.

Phin's boater blew off and ran to the end of its tether before he retrieved it. He and Brenda and Miss Pharaoh roared, over the roar of the wind, and after a moment even Martin's puritanical square shoulders shook with laughter.

After a pause, Phin asked casually, "And the footprint?"

"What?"

"The footprint, Miss Pharaoh. You said you and Martin were making a cast of a footprint in your garden. Isn't that evidence of some kind?"

"Perhaps. You'll see it, eventually, and you can decide for yourself."

"But what do you think of it?"

"I?" She made a face. "I intend not to be another Major Stokes, leaping to all possible conclusions. There must be a reason for this, and for all these other burglaries and vandalizations, and one reason only. It may have something to do with the Major's death or it may not, but I mean to find out everything."

"What other burglaries?" Martin asked. "You mean the Latimer—?"

Phin explained briefly the incidents of the orange, Yellow Pages, symbol for indigo and blue paint. "Along with the mysterious Mr Green and your aunt's violets, it makes an interesting spectrum, or almost."

"*Almost*," Miss Pharaoh repeated. "The missing colour is

red, and the only Unraveller unheard from is Frank Danby."

Brenda's eyes widened. "So that's the point of this great expedition today! But why didn't you just phone Mr Danby and—"

"I did." Miss Pharaoh began to twist the brim of her hat in her lap. "I phoned him yesterday, ostensibly to ask if he'd received my invitation, if he'd be coming to the reunion. He was—evasive. Said he *might* have received it, couldn't remember. But he had no intention of coming, and wouldn't say why. I gather that he wasn't exactly overjoyed at the idea of seeing the old gang."

"Did you tell him we might drop in today?" Phin asked.

"I hinted at it. But Frank fell all over himself trying to get out of it. He wasn't feeling well, he might be out . . . He's certainly acting fishy, if you ask me."

Martin winked at her over his shoulder. "Maybe it's because he lives by the sea?"

Brenda groaned, but the others ignored him.

"What about his background?" Phin asked. He opened his notebook to a fresh page. "What do you know about Frank Danby?"

"Very little, I'm afraid. Of course I knew him at the club in the old days, but everything since has been mere gossip."

"Such as?"

"You knew he was a policeman? As I understand it, he didn't just resign from the force, he was *asked* to resign. Evidently he was accused of beating a confession out of a suspect. There was an investigation, but nothing was proved."

"Typical," said Brenda. "I suppose his friends covered up for him, as usual."

Martin coughed. "That's not really fair, darling. By and large . . ." They settled down to an argument about the police, while the two sleuths in the back seat carried on with Danby's history.

"Anyway, there was enough suspicion of him to force his resignation. This was shortly after the war, I believe. Then he went to work for one of those security firms, guarding bank money or something of the sort—a firm calling itself the Trinkham Security Agency."

"But now he's retired?"

"Yes, a year ago, or was it two years? That's when he moved down to Dawson, a little village on the coast. He has a small cottage by the sea, he says. That's just about all I've been able to learn about him."

"You heard nothing about Major Stokes visiting him?"

"What? I don't believe it. The Major would never . . ."

Phin nodded, so vigorously that the boater slipped sideways. "So Gervase Hyde says. What's more, he says that Danby threatened to kill the Major."

"Did he indeed?" Miss Pharaoh was silent for a moment, while Brenda and Martin continued their wandering debate:

". . . and you're just impossible sometimes! I suppose next thing I'll hear that British justice is the best in the world! Honestly . . ."

". . . not what I said at all. Brenda, listen. I know there aren't many black policemen, but what's that got to do with . . ."

"There's a pub ahead," said Miss Pharaoh. "Let's all pull over and cool off, shall we? You two are bickering like an old married couple."

The pub had a garden, so that, while the adults from the procession sat bumping knees round a rusty table beneath a Martini umbrella, Mia Tavener was able to sit squirming on her mother's lap. Before the rest had even tasted their drinks, Mia had managed to kick over her glass of lemonade.

"Let the child go and play, for goodness' sake," said Miss Pharaoh. "There is something important I think you all should know about." She sipped at her lager until Mia had gone to torment a smaller child at the other end of the garden.

"What is it?" Hyde asked.

"First I'd like to hear your version of the meeting between Major Stokes and Frank Danby."

He drained his pint and wiped the foam from his moustache. "Not much to tell. The Major told me this about a month ago, when I ran into him quite by chance in Oxford Street. Said he went to visit Danby. As soon as he told him who he was, Danby turned nasty, ordered him off the place and said that if he ever caught him hanging about again, he'd kill him."

Leonard Latimer gasped. "Why didn't you mention this just now in the car, when I was talking about Stokes?"

Hyde grinned. "Didn't want to upset you while you were driving, old man. You're always going on about your heart— why take a chance?"

"Yes, but—" Latimer broke off and turned away, looking at his nails.

"That's not the point at all," said Miss Pharaoh. "The point is, why didn't Danby remember this when I spoke to him on the phone yesterday? To put it even more strongly, why did he lie about it?"

Phin asked what she meant.

"I didn't tell him the Major was dead, I simply asked Frank if he'd seen him recently." She put down her glass and watched a wasp trying to alight on the rim of it. "He *laughed*. It was that short, rather cruel laugh he always had. He laughed and said, 'Why no, Dorothea. I've not seen old Stokes since the war.' Then he made an excuse and rang off."

Phin watched how they took the news. Latimer swung back to face her, and immediately hid his hands. Martin and Brenda stopped their undertone argument to stare. Hyde shrugged and belched.

Derek Portman was more interesting. His over-sized actorish face underwent a series of adjustments, as though seeking the appropriate expression: anger? astonishment? delight (I-knew-it-all-along)? At length he settled for veiled suspicion.

"It's just enough, isn't it?" he said. "I certainly mean to ask Danby what—"

"We all want to ask him, Derek." Miss Pharaoh's dark eyes were solemn. "But we must go about this in the proper way. There may be some perfectly innocent explanation."

"Such as?"

"Maybe that he forgot about the visit. Or he might have been kidding, for some reason of his own."

Latimer put his hands away. "I n–never knew Danby to have a sense of humour, have you? I mean, he used to chuckle over those r–rape scenes in the gory novels he read, but that's no more a sense of humour than I'm a—"

"What I want to do," said Miss Pharaoh, "is see how he reacts to the news of Major Stokes's death—and that we think it's murder."

"Putting it a bit strong," said Latimer. "We've no more physical evidence than the man in the moon!"

Portman brought out his silver pencil and began doodling on the table. "What we've got is a lie. I, for one, would like to nail it down. So let's stop daydreaming, Latimer, and get going."

Everyone finished his drink except Miss Pharaoh. She sat mesmerized by the wasp, fluttering its cuneiform wings on the edge of her lager glass. At last it fell in.

"What are you thinking?" said Phin. "Is there something else about the Unravellers? Something you haven't told me?"

"Nothing like that," she confessed. "I was just making up another palindrome." She pointed to the glass. "*Regal wasp saw lager.*"

Dolphin Cottage, they found, was one of a row of identical white-washed brick bungalows set facing the lead-coloured sea. The road ran along behind them, past identical peeling kitchen doors and dented dustbins, to a weed-grown car park. They had two chances to view each house: once driving past the back, and once walking along the beach past the front. There was the shuttered and padlocked place, the clean place with window boxes, the deserted place, the place festooned with clotheslines and roaring with Radio One music, and so on—all of them unimposing, most of them squalid.

A chill breeze blew steadily from the sea. Miss Pharaoh shivered as she took her nephew's arm and led the promenade along the beach. From the front, a few of the cottages looked even more dismal, sprouting weeds from the cracks in their front steps.

On one set of steps sat a man facing the sea. He wore a garish purple shirt, open to the waist, ragged trousers, sunglasses and a vaguely nautical cap—but the kind sold at fun fairs. He was a big, hulking man with the battered face of an ex-boxer. Apparently Miss Pharaoh recognized the broken nose in profile, for she called out:

"Frank! Frank Danby! It's Dorothea, Frank. I said we might all of us drop by, and we have."

The man either did not hear or was practised at insult, for he continued to regard the water, his battered face turned to them in profile. As they drew closer, he took up a brass pocket telescope and studied the sea intently. Finally, without looking round, he said:

"Hullo, Dorothea. I notice you've brought the whole bloody gang with you after all. Thought I told you, didn't fancy having bloody visitors."

She stiffened. "See here, Frank, you're not a copper on duty any more, you might try being a bit human. After all, we've come down here to discuss something important."

"Important to you, maybe, but not—"

"It's important to you, too, Frank. May we go inside?"

He sighed. "Why not? But don't expect any VIP treatment, any of you." Without waiting to see if they followed, he shut the telescope, rose and went into the house.

They followed, and the tension went inside with them. The front door opened directly into a small lounge, hardly big enough to hold everyone. Danby, still wearing his cap and glasses, sprawled in the most comfortable-looking armchair. Miss Pharaoh introduced them all as they shuffled in and found places: Martin, Brenda, Latimer, Hyde, Phin, Portman, Sheila and Mia. Danby grunted at some names, blew down his nose at others, but said nothing.

Mia seemed to feel the tension immediately, and she asked to go out and play on the beach. Sheila trailed after her. The others, having disposed themselves about the room, stood or sat in silence.

Glimpses through the two open doors gave them a picture of the rest of the house: a tiny kitchen, a tinier bath, and the walls apparently papered throughout with the same pattern of faded yellow-green roses. Phin guessed without looking that there would be rust stains in the bath, soggy tea leaves in the kitchen sink, and a rent book among the wad of papers jammed behind the mantel clock. This was the "furnished accommodation" rented by someone long past caring about appearances.

The dilapidated lounge furniture, a few armchairs and wooden chairs and useless little tables, had all been shoved back against the walls, as through in preparation for dancing on the grimy lino. The four older guests sat stiffly against the walls, while Martin, Brent and Phin squatted near the front door. Everyone waited for the silence to break, while it grew more unbreakable by the minute.

Danby himself seemed indifferent to it. There was a kitchen hatch in the wall just above his head. He reached up and through it, found a can of beer and popped the top.

"Cheers," he said, his broken nose twisting a little as he smiled. "Sorry there's only enough for me." He swigged it noisily as he closed the hatch.

"Don't be so damned childish, Frank," said Miss Pharaoh. "We didn't expect . . . Good heavens, what was that?"

From behind a closed door they heard a sudden flurry of scratching and snarling. The door shook as a huge weight crashed against it.

"That? That's Sheba, my little Alsatian. Only thing wakes her up is when I open a can of beer. She's crazy about it. *Sheba, lie down!* Yes, lucky for all of you I happened to have her shut in the bedroom, eh? She'd as soon take an arm off a stranger as look at them. Like to meet her?" He made a move as though to rise, then fell back laughing.

Portman said, "I've had about enough of this. If you want to sit swilling beer and playing cruel games with your dog, go ahead. I've always said, the only thing that makes a dog nasty is a nasty owner. If the rest of you want to sit here playing games with this —this lunatic, all right, but count me out."

Danby said, "You were counted out a long time ago, Portman. Just sit down and enjoy this bloody reunion or whatever it's supposed to be."

Miss Pharaoh said, "Frank, listen. Stokes is dead. I have reason to believe he's been murdered."

Danby sucked at the beer can. "So?"

"Is that all you've got to say? 'So'?"

"What do you want me to do, start playing detectives with you? What do I care about what happens to old Stokes? Got my own bloody life to leave—to live."

"There are one or two things you might explain," Portman said. "Such as why you said you hadn't seen Stokes in twenty years, when he came to talk to you about a month ago."

Danby's face, in so far as its scarred rigidity allowed, showed a flash of surprise. "Told you that, did he? Tell you how I threatened to set Sheba on him if he didn't piss off?" Once more the vicious laugh. "Oh, I see. You think I—ha ha—you think I'd *bother* to rub that old bastard out? Christ—and this is some kind of a little kangaroo court, is that it?"

"He said you threatened him," said Portman. "I don't see any joke in that. You threatened a man's life and now he's dead. Is that funny?"

"You're funny. All of you. You want my alibi for the time of death? I was right here. Right here in this house, or not more than a hundred yards away. Is that where he died?"

Miss Pharaoh said, "No, in London. But how do you know *when* he died?"

"Makes no difference. I've been here every day for the past year. *Never* go out, told you that on the phone."

"Sounds a bit gangsterish," said Hyde. "What's all this talk about rubbing people out and never going anywhere? What are you hiding from?"

"None of your fucking business!"

Suddenly Latimer was on his feet, his jowls shaking with rage. "How dare you use language like that in front of Dorothea and my daughter? How dare you? I've half a mind to—"

"To 'teach me a lesson'? You never were man enough, Latimer, so sit down and shut up."

"Stop shouting, both of you." Miss Pharaoh looked at Latimer until he sat down. "Now, Frank. We hadn't meant this to be entirely a social call. You see, whatever happened to Major Stokes seems to involve all of us."

Danby nodded. "Maybe you'd better tell me the whole story."

"All right. But we may as well have something to eat while we talk. Martin, will you fetch in the hamper?"

Phin stood up to let him pass. Then, while Miss Pharaoh explained, he wandered about the room looking for some clue to Danby's strange animosity.

Over the fireplace hung a dust-covered photo of Danby, a few years younger and dressed in the paramilitary uniform of the Trinkham Security Agency: peaked cap, sunglasses, elaborate jacket and trousers and shiny boots. One hand rested on the hilt of a heavy truncheon, while the other restrained a large, vicious-looking dog.

Below on the mantel shelf there was little of interest: an old clock without a crystal, a wad of envelopes and papers jammed behind it, and a cheap transistor radio. Keeping his back to the ex-policeman, Phin slid a few items out from behind the clock and looked them over. They were unopened letters.

Martin came in with the huge wicker hamper and set it down in the middle of the floor. "I looked for Sheila and Mia," he said. "No sign of them. I expect they've wandered off down the beach somewhere. But there was a funny thing about the water . . ."

"Never mind," said Miss Pharaoh. "There's a big flask of tea in there, and some bread and things. If you and Brenda can find a knife and start cutting sandwiches, I'd like to finish what I was saying." She turned to Danby. "Where was I? Oh—after Stokes's death, there began a series of puzzling little incidents . . ."

Phin made himself useful, finding a bread knife in the kitchen while Brenda and Martin knelt and began unloading the hamper.

"Funny thing," Martin said in a half-whisper. "Just out front there—some kind of pollution in the water."

Phin bent to hand the knife to Brenda. "What kind of pollution?"

"Red stuff. A kind of red oil slick or something. Almost looks like blood."

CHAPTER NINE

"Is it important?" Brenda asked, seeing Phin's face.

"Important! *Important!*" Phin straightened up. "It's what I've been waiting for. Listen, everyone. Martin's just seen something."

"Red stuff," Martin said. "Red stuff in the water."

There was an instant of silence while they took it in, and then a mad rush to the door. Phin and Martin led the way and the others followed, down the cracked steps and across the broad gravel beach to the water's edge.

"I've never seen anything like it," said Brenda.

A dozen yards out, one enormous patch of water had turned bright red. The incoming tide moved it gently, causing it to swirl and spread.

"Can't be blood," Latimer puffed. "Take a whale to give out that much. Must be twenty yards across? Thirty?"

"What in God's name is it?" Portman asked. "Red oil? And why—?"

Gervase Hyde shrugged. "Paint, maybe? Think I'll get uphill where I can see it better. Seems to be a hell of a lot of it." He started back towards the house.

"Pollution was what I thought," said Martin. "Of course there wasn't so much of it when I looked before."

Latimer sat down and started struggling with his shoelaces, as Miss Pharaoh joined the group.

"Think I'll just try wading out and collecting a sample," he said. "The water doesn't look deep here."

They watched him roll up his trousers over heavy white calves before stepping cautiously into the lapping waves.

Miss Pharaoh stood a little apart from the others, the breeze ruffling her white hair. Phin called to her:

"Are you all right, Miss Pharaoh? You look a bit distracted."

"What? Yes, of course. I'm only thinking what I suppose you are thinking."

"Yes. This completes the cycle. Green for Stokes, orange for Portman, yellow for Latimer, indigo for Hyde, violet for you, blue for Sir Tony Fitch, and now red for Danby." He walked over to her and lowered his voice. "Convenient that we're all here to see it, isn't it?"

She called to her nephew. "Martin, would you do me a favour? Run up to the house and fetch . . . Oh, never mind."

Martin shrugged and stayed put.

Latimer found the water too deep, turned and waded back. Gervase Hyde came back down to the shore, shaking his head. And now their crowd began to attract people from neighbouring houses, who ambled down to stare at the phenomenon. Phin looked among them for Sheila or Mia Taverner, but in vain.

"I see the tide's coming in," Martin said. "Maybe a ship dumped its cargo at sea, or something like that. Ever see anything like this, Mr Phin?"

"No, and somehow I can't believe it's accidental pollution."

Miss Pharaoh watched Latimer sitting down to tie his shoes. He'd left them too close to the water's edge, and they were soaked. "No, I don't think it's accidental at all. The colour is simply too convenient. This can only be a message for Frank. The same message we've all received."

"Oh, *that*." Martin looked dubious. "That business you were explaining in the car? But I still don't see what the point is."

"That," said Miss Pharaoh, "is exactly what's so fascinating about it. Are we being warned off or led on? And why? It's a tidy little puzzle—"

"By the way—" Martin looked round— "I don't see Mr Danby."

Latimer struggled to his feet. "Never came out of the house. Sulking again, I expect."

"I wonder if he's all right. Let's go see."

Phin started after them, but Miss Pharaoh restrained him. "There's something else, you know. Stokes was always going on about . . . He had one favourite expression. He—"

A deeply tanned little man with bulging eyes appeared before them, offering Phin his grubby hand. "Gall's the name, Fred Gall. Down here for your holidays, are you?"

"How do you do, Mr Gall."

"Me and the missus always comes down this time of year. Not so crowded, you know? Mind you the weather's not been so good this year. Next year I think we'll take a caravan to Torquay, you know?"

"Mr Gall, have you ever seen anything like that before in these parts?" Phin pointed at the red patch.

"Naw, but then nothink surprises me. Shocking, the filth they throw in here. Arab oil ships, I expect. Dump any old rubbish on us, what do they care? Shocking. On the whole, though, it's nice here. Mind you, the telly here's not like at home. Reception's shocking. Must be the electrical interference of the sea. Waves and all."

"Shocking," Phin murmured. "You didn't by any chance see a woman with a small girl anywhere about, a few minutes ago?"

"Your missus, is it? Naw, I was watching 'Grandstand'. But the missus might know where they went. I'll go ask her, okay?"

"Thank you, Mr Gall." Phin watched him go, then turned to Miss Pharaoh. "The Major's favourite expression?"

"Yes, he kept going on about a Red Tide. Naturally I thought he meant the usual metaphor, but now . . ."

She looked out at the pink-tinged tide, just as Latimer shouted from the house.

"Come quickly! Danby's hurt—I think he's dead!"

The figures on the beach all remained motionless for a heart-beat, then all moved at once. Hyde reached the house first, with Phin bounding up the steps behind him.

Frank Danby sat much as before, in the same chair. He'd slipped down a few inches and the back of the chair had pushed

93

his head forward, so that he seemed to be staring at the great black projection under his chin. It was the handle of a knife, and enough of the serrated blade projected to identify it as his own bread knife.

Martin stood by, paralysed. "I tried to pull it out, but it's st–stuck! Oh my God, what shall we do?" His voice was high-pitched with hysteria.

Latimer was hardly any better off. Blanched, gasping for breath as though he too had been stabbed in the throat, he lurched wildly about the room, stumbling at every other step on his untied shoelaces.

Hyde simply stared. "Can't be alive," he kept saying. "He just can't be alive!"

Phin felt for a pulse. "He's not."

Sergeant Bevis of the local CID stood on the front steps to address the crowd of witnesses waiting on the gravel below. "Now you've all told your stories to me or to one of my men. I'll have to ask some of you to remain for further questioning." He stood aside to let two ambulance men come out carrying a plastic coffin.

"The following people may go home now: Mr and Mrs Gall, Mr Patel, Mrs Nelson. Thank you for your help." He stood aside again as two men carried out Danby's armchair, swathed in poly-thene. A uniformed policeman came next, leading a large, toothy Alsatian dog. The policeman's heavy gloves were torn. The dog came reluctantly, snapping at its chain.

"So this is the dog, is it?" asked Bevis unnecessarily.

"Yes, sir. You must have heard the row she kicked up when I went in for her. Had to give her a tranquillizer."

In the crowd, Phin turned back to his conversation with a large woman wearing pink hair curlers. "This is most enlighten-ing, Mrs Gall. You're absolutely sure?"

"Well, I saw her with my own eyes . . ."

Phin and the other detained witnesses were asked to drive to the station in Brogham, a town fourteen miles away. When they got there, it was only to be kept waiting for another two hours,

94

until the people from Scotland Yard were ready to speak to them. The interrogations went on for hours, and it was after dark when Thackeray Phin was finally called in to face Chief Inspector Gaylord.

"Sit down, Phin. I hope you know the local lads are annoyed with you. This Sergeant Bevis wanted to charge you with being a damn nuisance and hindering the police."

Phin took a chair, folded his hands over the handle of his green umbrella, and rested his chin on them. "I haven't hindered anyone. If anything, I've been speeding up the investigation."

Gaylord unwrapped a cigar and ran it beneath his hawk-beak nose. "Oh, solved it all, have you? Then maybe you'd condescend to tell us the answer."

"The answer?" Phin looked blank. "Oh, who killed him, you mean? That's your department, Chief. I wouldn't dream of interfering. No, I've been trying to answer a few other questions: Why, for instance, did the killer take such a terrible risk? I mean, there were so many people there, going in and out of that room at odd times—it was very chancy."

"So I thought. Seems to me the killer was very desperate, willing to take any risk, rather than let Danby live. The trouble is . . ."

"The trouble is, you can't find any suspect with such a desperate motive, I imagine. Neither can I, Chief, neither can I. And in that case, it could be a successful murder. The killer achieved his object."

Gaylord lit his cigar and chewed at it a moment. "I don't believe in successful murders, do you? Someone in your little mob has a connection with Danby, and I mean to find out that connection. Now, what I want from you is your opinion of the suspects. Who do you think' would and could kill Danby?"

"*Would* kill him? Almost anyone. To know him was to detest him. *Could* kill him? That narrows it down considerably. In our group I can think of four people only: the last person who left the house, the first person who returned, and the two persons seen near it in the meantime."

"And who might those four persons be?"

"That's what I'm not sure about. I talked to a neighbour, a Mrs Gall, who says she saw a woman *sneaking* round to the back of the house. She pointed the woman out to me: Sheila Taverner. This was after she says she saw Gervase Hyde *skulking* near the front door. So that makes two suspects."

Gaylord puffed in silence for a time before he said: "We're aware of those two. But we're having a problem finding out who was the last one out or the first one in."

"I know what you mean: Miss Pharaoh thought she was the last one out of the room, but then she remembered Brenda Latimer going back with—I quote—'a knife in her hand'. Brenda seems to agree, and she thinks she laid the knife down somewhere, but can't remember where. Let's hope she didn't leave it in Mr Danby's throat."

Gaylord puffed some more. "Tell me, Phin, when you left the house, were the kitchen door and hatch closed?"

"Yes. Danby closed the hatch after fetching out his beer. I closed the door myself, when I came out with the knife, earlier. I can't help closing doors, it's my one habit of tidiness."

"They're still closed," said Gaylord. Squinting through the cigar haze, he added: "I'm not satisfied at all. Having the whole house gone over for prints hasn't given us a hell of a lot to work on. Everybody's prints are in the front room, and nobody's but Danby's in the rest of the house. Except—"

Phin leaned forward slightly. "Except what?"

"Except a partial one on the handle of the back door. Not Danby's, but we haven't been able to match it to any of the others either. The lads are still working on it."

"Chief, let me see if I can read your mind. You suspect that Sheila Taverner went round the back, in the back door, and did the deed?"

"Could be. Sheila Taverner or someone else. Let's just suppose that Brenda Latimer left the knife in the kitchen. And the back door leads straight into the kitchen. Say Sheila nips round back, goes in, snatches up the knife and . . . There are three ways she could get to Danby. She could go into the front room. She could open the door and reach round and stab him. Or she could open

96

the little sliding doors of the hatch, lean through and stab him from above."

"But surely your prints would tell you—"

"Pair of rubber gloves in the kitchen, available to anyone."

"I see." Phin chewed his lip. "What about her motive?"

"We're lucky again. Miss Taverner has form. Been done a few years ago for shoplifting. And guess which security firm caught her at it?"

"Not—"

"Right: the Trinkham Security Agency. We're checking further, and if we find that the name of the officer who nicked her was Frank Danby . . . Hey, don't stab your umbrella into the floor like that! It makes marks."

"Sorry. So you suspect Sheila Taverner, Gervase Hyde, Brenda Latimer and—how about Miss Pharaoh? I suppose she's out of it?"

"Yes, if Brenda took the knife into the house after she left, she's clear. Hang that umbrella up, will you? Gets on my nerves."

Phin hung it on the edge of the desk and folded his arms. "Then we have Martin Hughes and Leonard Latimer. Could one or both of them have done it?"

"*I'm* supposed to be questioning *you*, remember? But for your information, they claim to have found the body together. They're hazy as hell about the details, but that's not unusual. I don't think there's much chance that one of them rushed in first and stabbed him, or anything like that. And that seems to dispose of your little group. You and Portman were on the beach continuously, according to all witnesses."

"Glad to hear it," said Phin. "But you know, there's another possibility. Have you considered outsiders?"

"Outsiders? Of course that's possible, but—"

"But listen. No one ever looked into that bedroom, which opens right off the front room. We were all told there was a savage dog in there. But suppose Sheba wasn't alone?"

"Someone hiding in the bedroom, eh? They nip out, stab Danby and run. Hmm. How would they get into the bedroom?"

"Isn't there a window in it? On the side of the house?"

Gaylord stubbed out his cigar. "Yes, but no one went in or out of that window. The sill's thick with dust."

"All right then, how's this? Danby himself hid this person in the bedroom. That would explain why he was so anxious to get rid of all of us—and why he failed to come out to look at the red stuff in the water."

A constable knocked and came in with a sheaf of papers. He and Gaylord whispered together for a moment.

"Well, well. Thank you, Constable. Phin, I don't think we'll need to worry about your 'outsider' just yet. First, we'll be going over your little group again, eh? I mean, no point in looking much further, just now. These final fingerprint reports make fascinating reading."

"I'd love to read them myself, if—"

"Hands off. Let's just say we've confirmed your prints on the door between the kitchen and front room, so your story holds up."

Phin stared at him. "Chief, *that*'s not what's got you so excited. What else have you found? That partial print on the back door . . ."

"Yes, we've indentified it. I won't say whose it is, but let's just say Miss Sheila Taverner will continue helping us with our enquiries. You may go, Phin."

Phin stood up. "I think you're making a mistake."

"Do you, now?"

"Yes, I do. I mean, why was Danby acting like a recluse in the first place? Mrs Gall said he never went anywhere, had his groceries delivered, never spoke to anyone when he met them on the beach—she said he acted like a gangster hiding out from the law. And we've all seen that dog of his."

"Yes? So what?"

"Are you seriously suggesting, Chief, that Frank Danby was scared, scared into hiding—by Sheila Taverner?"

CHAPTER TEN

BY MIDNIGHT IT WAS COLD. In the fireplace of Miss Pharaoh's spacious study, a fire was blazing, and so were the tempers of the assembled company.

They had shuffled in, exhausted from travelling and from the nerve-grinding events of the day. Still, as Latimer quipped unconsciously, they were willing to "take a stab at anything". Accordingly the ugly Queen Anne chairs and the old leather chesterfield were dragged into a fireside group, and the discussion began.

So far they were each taking a stab at the other. Phin found his attention wandering. He gazed about in the dimly lit space, seeing faces and objects as though for the first time.

Latimer sat next to the fire, holding out his hands to it, but not as though to warm them. Rather, he seemed to be trying to get a better look at them, and not to care at all for what he saw. The orange firelight blasted up at him, throwing the huge shadows of his fingers up, across his face.

Portman sat next to him, his hands and feet crossed, his large face immobile. It was always thus when he wasn't speaking: he looked like nothing so much as a large puppet, awaiting the cue that would bring it to life. Yet the half-closed eyes were watchful.

Hyde was sprawled, all but snoring. The shadows of the ends of his bandit's moustache moved, as the flickering light moved them only. Though his face was motionless, a phantom smile seemed sometimes to play across it.

Martin and Brenda were up and moving about, unpacking the lunch hamper and trying to find something in it still edible. The further they moved from the light, the more Phin found his gaze following them, seeking them out in the shadows. The close-cropped dark head and the straw-coloured blonde one—were they whispering together conspiratorially, over by the old roll-top desk in the corner? Every gesture seemed sinister: Martin picking up a tissue-wrapped packet; Brenda turning her face from the light . . .

And in the fireside circle, Miss Pharaoh herself seemed sinister, as she chatted lightly with Portman. The solicitor turned his great head and nodded, as though her words had stirred him into life by their significance.

But she was only speaking of logical fallacies:

". . . as you should know, Derek, the absence of disproof is no proof. There's the story of the man being tried for theft, and the prosecution called four witnesses who saw him do it. He then called eight witnesses who *hadn't* seen him do it!" the gold tooth gleamed.

I must be tired, Phin accused himself. *Suspecting everyone . . .*

It was then that they began the argument which quickly showed how tired and irritable everyone was.

"Look," said Portman, "I don't want any stale sandwiches or cold tea, thank you, Brenda. And I don't want any leftover theories, either. Why don't we just do what we came here to do, thrash this thing out?"

Hyde stirred himself. "All a question of motive, old man."

"*Motive?*" Latimer's hands shook, until he flipped them out of sight in the shadows. "Don't dodge the issue by putting up a smoke screen, Hyde. Motive's as plain as a pikestaff, for pity's sake! Everyone hated Frank Danby's guts!"

Phin said, "If I could suggest—"

"The man in the moon's got motive! We want to get down to brass tacks. The *fact* is, Hyde, you were near the damned house for at least five min—"

Portman said, "But Danby was dead already, don't you see? Once we examine alibis and—"

"All of you are pathetic!" Miss Pharaoh shouted. "Listen to yourselves. This has to be reasoned out, and you're all going on like a pack of gibbering orangutans. The proof—"

"Your proof?" said Portman. "With an alibi like yours, I could prove just about anything."

Phin said, "I'd like to suggest—"

"Dad, do you want a sandwich?"

"How can I eat, listening to this *motive* rubbish, this *alibi* rubbish, this *reasoning* rubbish. Without facts—"

"Listen for a while, Latimer, No point trying to bully us with facts, while Dorothea sits here smugly—"

"Aunt Dorothea, I think Mr Phin's trying to get a word in."

"I'd like to suggest we calm down and—"

"Good idea, Phin. If we take the facts calmly, the answer is obvious. Plain as a pike—"

"Whenever you're through gargling clichés, Latimer, I just want to say—"

"Daddy, you really ought to eat something. It'll calm you."

"I am calm! I am calm, damn it!"

Latimer stood up and flung a plate to the floor. It made no sound on the thick carpet, but the silent violence of it hit them. No one spoke for a moment, until Miss Pharaoh said drily:

"Obviously, Leonard, you are calm as a pikestaff."

The laugh semed to drain them of all the tension and horror of the day's ordeal. Miss Pharaoh asked Martin and Brenda to take away the picnic leftovers and bring out coffee and brandy. Then she turned to Phin.

"Our poor sleuth here has been trying to get a word in edgeways."

"I was just going to suggest that we take it in turns, without arguing. Everyone here seems to have a theory, and I'd like to hear them all."

"Excellent. Who'll start? Gervase?"

Hyde poured himself a generous brandy and downed it. "That's better." He wiped his moustache. "Let me say first of all that the police are dead wrong. I must admit there's a certain attractiveness about their notion, but—no, it's too fantastic. No one goes about carrying a grudge over—what was it? shoplifting?—and waiting for a remote chance like this. So we have to look elsewhere. But which of us had the opportunity? I had, Brenda

Latimer had, and perhaps Latimer and Hughes together had."

"If you're going to accuse my daughter, I think you might wait until she's back in the room," said Latimer.

"But I'm not accusing her. What possible motive could she have? Nor Martin Hughes either. And that leaves thee and me, Latimer. Now both of us knew Danby and disliked him, even hated him perhaps. But neither of us is a fool. If you had wanted to kill him, I'm quite certain you could have rigged up some untraceable poison and slipped it in his can of beer or something. No, this is an impulsive crime, the crime of a rash fool. So you couldn't have done it, and I know I didn't, so that eliminates all of us. Frank Danby was murdered by an outsider."

"That's no good," said Latimer. "We—"

"Wait, let me finish. Let's take this crime in connection with the death of Major Stokes. That is said to be murder again, and that points to a common motive. Someone had reason to kill both men, and yet that someone was not one of the Unravellers.

"The answer isn't hard to find, once we look at the characters of the two dead men. Both were recluses, secretive men. Stokes was known for his habit of collecting information on people, 'getting the goods on them' as he used to call it. Danby was known for his cruelty and sadism. But a nosy sadist is what they make up together, and a nosy sadist is, by definition, a blackmailer."

Miss Pharaoh snorted, but said nothing.

"Now we ask ourselves, which of us could be blackmailed? Not me, my life's an open, if soiled, book. Not you, Dorothea. Your life, if you'll forgive my saying so, is rather a blank page. You, Latimer? No, we all know your little secret, and I see no possibility for blackmail there."

He turned to Portman. "But your case is rather different, is it not? At least from what I've heard, you have a rather dubious chapter in your book."

Portman said, "Mind the slander laws, Hyde, and remember you're talking to a lawyer."

"Just a moment." Phin held up a hand. "If you want us to continue the discussion, Mr Portman, I think you ought to waive your right to sue anyone for slander. So must we all, for tonight, or this investigation comes to a dead stop."

"Agreed," said Portman finally. Out came the notebook and silver pencil, and he began a furious doodle as Hyde went on.

"We know that Sir Tony Fitch opposed the attentions that were being paid to his only daughter by a young law clerk named Portman. He was so opposed that he arranged his will to prevent any marriage between them. Or at least to prevent Derek Portman from benefiting from such a marriage."

The doodle stopped. "How the devil did you know that?"

"Gossip from old Stokes, actually. I told you he was nosy. And we had quite a chat that day in Oxford Street. Shall I go on?"

Portman underwent the peculiar shift of expressions Phin had seen earlier, his large, mobile face finally settling into a rather overdone neutrality. "Of course. I have nothing to hide."

About the room, people shifted in the uncomfortable Queen Anne chairs.

"The terms of the will were these: if Pamela was married to Portman at the time of her father's death, she got his London house, his country house, and a few sticks of furniture. But if they were not married, she inherited his considerable fortune.

"Now comes the problem. Sir Tony's London house was bombed in the blitz, and his daughter identified a mangled body as his. She then immediately married young Portman. Obviously they'd only been waiting for Sir Tony to kick off. Trouble was, he wasn't dead, was he?"

"I have nothing to say on the subject." Portman tried a bored expression. "You carry on with your twisted version."

"A twist of irony, eh? A few days after the marriage, a man died in Charing Cross Hospital. He'd been found wandering the streets in a semi-comatose condition from a head wound, and not able to talk. Since he was wearing pyjamas and no dentures, and since no one stepped forward to claim him, identification had been impossible. But of course after death, the police made more enquiries and learned his identity. It was Sir Tony.

"There was a lot of money involved, so of course there were a lot of questions. The coroner wanted to know whose the original

103

body was, didn't he, Portman? The police wanted to know how Sir Tony had come by that head injury. And I imagine that the Law Society wanted to know how a member had become ensnarled in such a shady-sounding affair."

Miss Pharaoh interrupted. "All most entertaining, Gervase, but hardly enlightening. Are you accusing Derek of some sort of funny business with the bodies? Or even of murder?"

Hyde shrugged. "Who knows what really happened? Stokes? Danby? They're dead, so the secret may very well be buried for ever. My point is, the police have shown that anyone could have slipped in the back way to stab Danby. And possibly the Hon. Pamela Fitch-Portman has an excellent motive, protecting her inheritance. How does that sound?"

Portman had listened to the last part of this with his hands half covering his face. Now they covered it completely, as his shoulders quivered and he made peculiar snuffling noises.

"Derek, what is it?" asked Miss Pharaoh.

Portman raised his large face, to show everyone that he was convulsed with silent laughter. Finally he caught his breath and roared, "How does it sound? How does it—ah ha ha—excuse me, that's the best—the best confabulation I've ever heard outside a courtroom. Hyde, you ought to have read for the bar."

He wiped his eyes and accepted a glass of brandy from Martin. "Thanks. I suppose I should explain what really happened. The bit about the will is substantially correct. Stokes ought to know, since he was one of the witnesses to Sir Tony's will. As for the rest, I hardly know where to begin refuting it. The fact is, Pamela and I had no designs on the old boy's money, as he thought. We obtained a special licence to marry and told him so. And—here's the funny part—he relented! He was about to draw up a new will giving Pamela everything, without conditions. But he was bombed."

"So you say," Hyde murmured.

"You don't see it, do you? Under the terms of the old will, the very fact that we *applied* for a marriage licence was enough to spoil it for us. It doesn't matter who died when or where, we lost everything but the country house. In a sense, we no longer have even that. Now where's our motive for murder gone?"

"But why were you in such a hurry to get married after he died?"

"That," said Portman, "is apparently something neither Stokes nor you would understand. I've said all I have to say for now."

"I think I understand, Derek." Miss Pharaoh stirred her coffee. "But have you a theory on Frank's murder yourself?"

"Of course. Motive is a rubbishy way to approach this, anyway. Let's look at alibis. Unless he or she is demented, the murderer must have one, and we ought to discover where he or she is lying.

"First, let's dismiss those who have no alibis: Brenda Latimer, Leonard Latimer, Sheila Taverner and Martin Hughes. And I'd like to dismiss the notion of a convenient outsider, too.

"So it comes down to those with alibis: Mr Phin, myself, and you, Dorothea. Mr Phin and I have perfect alibis. We were not the last to leave the house, nor the first to return to it. In the meantime, both of us were seen to be on the beach, continuously.

"But you, Dorothea, have a rather contrived alibi. You say you saw Brenda going back into the house after you left. You say she was carrying the murder weapon. Brenda backs you up. But *we have only your word and hers for this.* No one else saw which of you left the house last. Now, since Brenda is about to marry your nephew, it is quite plausible for her to lie to protect you."

"I didn't lie!" said Brenda. "I rushed out with the knife in my hand, and then I ran back and—'"

"*And what?* You can't remember where you put the knife down. Could that be because you never had the knife? You never put it anywhere, because you didn't go back?"

Brenda looked the picture of innocence, with her wide blue eyes and turned-up nose, as she tried to stammer out a reply Miss Pharaoh came to her rescue.

"For heaven's sake, Derek, stop badgering the poor girl. If you have a point to make, simply make it."

"Since you insist," he said. "I find it curious that you've

remained a spinster all these years. We all fancied you a bit, you know, in the old days. I remember even old Sir Tony, in his bumbling and rather courtly way, trying to make time with you. But I also happen to know that Frank Danby fancied you."

"You're joking."

"I'm not. I can't help but wonder if he didn't try paying you the supreme compliment—in his own brutish way, of course."

Miss Pharaoh blushed. "I don't know what you're driving at."

"It's simple. I submit that Danby tried to rape you, at one time or other, and that the experience fairly well turned you off men for life. I see you shake your head. Well, no matter what you say, I imagine any meeting between you and Danby as the irresistible force meeting the immovable object. No?

"But let us follow that line of reasoning anyway, and see where it leads us. You conceive the notion of killing him, so you arrange a reunion. Stokes figures out your motive and confronts you with it on the phone, so you kill him. Then you whip up a few false trails and herrings of various colours, but all the while you're really planning this trip to Sussex, to get Danby. *You* arranged the trip, just as *you* arranged your alibi with Brenda. It's all succeeded, and I congratulate you."

Miss Pharaoh opened her mouth, closed it, finally said, "Derek, you must think me a complete ninny. Do you suppose for a moment I'd arrange a murder to implicate two innocent persons? Would I make Brenda my accomplice and throw the worst suspicion on poor Sheila? I certainly would not. I hope I'm a bit cleverer than that.

"I also hope I'm too clever to fling wild accusations about. So I won't tell you who killed either Major Stokes or Frank Danby. But I will tell you who did not:

"First, I assume one murderer for both crimes. That eliminates Leonard and Vera Latimer, who were out of the country when Stokes died. It eliminates Sheila and me, who were together when he died. It eliminates Mr Phin and Derek Portman, and Martin, none of whom can have killed Frank."

Hyde said, "Wait a minute. That leaves only me!"

"Or an outsider, Gervase. Or else it means I have assumed wrongly. These murders may have been performed by more than one person—in short, a conspiracy."

Martin snickered. "And you said the Major was crazy!"

"Oh, I don't mean a Red conspiracy, simply an agreement to commit murder. I say nothing of motives or alibis, but simply stick to the possible patterns: First, Gervase did the murders. Second, an outsider did them. Third, a conspiracy did them. But I believe it should be possible to find out which is the truth."

Latimer wiped a hand over his forehead. "I think we shouldn't try forcing the facts into patterns, but let them speak for themselves. Hyde, you hated both Stokes and Danby, so you have 'motive'—and even if you didn't, you're just about alcoholic enough and insane enough to try anything. As for alibi, you have none. All the same, I won't accuse you, because—because I think Sheila Taverner must have done it after all.

"Look at the case against her: She was seen going round the back of the house, they found her fingerprint on the back door; she lied about it too, I understand. And we know she had an old grudge against the Trinkham Security Agency, where Danby worked.

"Besides that, everyone keeps talking about it being an impulsive crime, a demented crime, a quick and foolish act. That fits, too. Sheila saw that photo of Danby in his uniform, it brought back all the old hatred, and—she went berserk."

Portman mumbled something.

"What was that?"

"Nothing, go on."

"That's my case, and you'll have to admit it's pretty strong."

Miss Pharaoh said, "It could hardly be weaker. Sheila was arrested for petty pilfering, shoplifting, several years ago. She is not demented, so I fail to see why she should kill a perfect stranger over such a trifle, years later. Especially now. She has paid for her crime, she has a decent job and a home, and she's busy bringing up her daughter. No, fingerprints or not, she simply cannot have done it."

"That's emotion talking," said Latimer. "Not logic."

"Oh, it's logic, too. We must assume that Sheila was intelligent enough to use rubber gloves to open the kitchen hatch and handle the weapon. How then can she have been so careless as to leave a print on the back door? It makes no sense at all."

Brenda spoke up. "I don't think I left that knife in the kitchen. I'm sure I left it in the front room. Wouldn't that clear Sheila?"

Portman smiled. "If I were your solicitor, young lady, I would advise you not to change your story now—unless you're absolutely sure. It might look . . . See what I mean?"

Martin sighed. "It all happened so fast, I guess we're all in the soup. When I found the body—"

"You found him first?" Phin asked. "Before Mr Latimer?"

"No," said Latimer. "We found him together. I'm pretty clear on that, at least."

"You didn't look too clear on anything when I saw you." Phin turned to Martin again. "What do you remember?"

"I went in first, I'm almost certain. I was just—I was paralysed when I saw him. I just stood there. Then Mr Latimer said 'Do something!' so I went over and tried to pull the thing out of him—it seemed stuck!"

"You probably just went weak from shock," said Phin. "I'm afraid all you did was spoil the prints on the handle."

"I know it was stupid, but . . . I thought he might be saved, somehow, if I could only get the damned knife out of him."

"There we have it, then," said Portman. "Nearly any of us could have done it. Seems to me we've wasted an evening's discussion. I—*my God!*"

Like two silent ghosts, a madonna-ghost carrying a child-ghost, Sheila and Mia Taverner drifted into the room.

Sheila stood uncertainly, looking at the shock in their faces. "They let us go," she said. "I mean, they let me go. Excuse me, I didn't mean to barge in. I'll just put Mia to bed and—"

"You'll sit down here," said Brenda. "I'll put Mia to bed. You must be dead tired, poor kid. Have a drink or something." There were minutes of electric activity, everyone trying to help the young woman, everyone trying not to ask the question that was uppermost in their minds. After they had given her a soft chair and a softer cushion, a cigarette and a glass of brandy, Miss Pharaoh finally asked:

"What changed their minds at last, Sheila?"

"Oh, I don't know for sure. I think they checked out my record, found out I didn't know Mr Danby from anywhere. And they found out what I was pinched for—taking one bloody packet of sugar. Oh yeah, and I told them about going into the kitchen, what I heard and all."

Miss Pharaoh knelt down before the girl. "Would you tell us the whole story? It would be such a help, Sheila."

"Okay, well." Sheila snuffled. "See, Mia and I went out on the beach. I lay down for a bit, and she . . . I suppose I must have dozed off or something, and she ran away.

"Well, I went looking for her, some way down the beach. And I was coming back when I saw all of you down on the beach, looking in the water. I thought, 'My God, she's drowned!' So I started towards you, then I saw Mia dodge back between the houses. So I went after her. I went right past Mr Hyde, only behind him, like, so I guess he didn't notice me. I went round to the back—no sign of her. Oh, she can be a little bugger when she wants. I saw Mr Danby's back door was open, so I thought, 'Aha!' and sneaked in. No sign of her! I was really going crazy by then. I was still looking round when I heard something in the front room."

A certain cheerfulness had crept over her in narrating the hide-and-seek game. Now it dropped away; she looked as haggard as when she'd drifted in. "I heard footsteps, and Mr Danby saying: 'Who the hell are you? What do you want?' Then he—he made this horrible gagging noise.

"I just turned and ran."

Phin cleared his throat. "Weren't you worried that Mia might be in the front room? That she might be in danger?"

"I just didn't think at all! I mean—everyone had been talking about murder—and that sound . . . I just panicked. I ran out in the road and tried to yell for Mia. Only my voice was all choked up, like, I could hardly make a sound. And then she sneaked up behind me and said 'Boo, Mummy!' I was never so glad to see anybody in my life. I just started to cry." She almost started now, but sniffed back the tears and continued:

"Then I heard Mr Latimer yelling that somebody was dead, so we went round to the front, and there was already a big mob coming up to the house. I felt safe then, with the crowd."

"Remarkable," said Hyde. "An ear-witness account!"

Phin was more cautious. "You're absolutely sure it was Danby's voice you heard? After all, you hadn't heard much of it before."

"I'm sure. The police asked me a lot about that, too. And they kept on at me about the footsteps. Were they high heels? Did they limp? Heavy or light? I kept telling them there was nothing special, they were just footsteps. I don't even know if it was a man or woman. I'd like to go to bed now."

"Just one question," said Phin. "Did you see anyone else at the back of the houses? In the road? Anyone at all?"

"No."

"Nice of you to give me a lift home, Mr Portman." Phin fastened his seat belt and leaned back in Rolls-Royce luxury.

"No trouble. I've got a fair drive to my own place, anyway. Tell me, what did you think of Miss Taverner's performance? You believe her?"

"I really don't know what to believe, with all the sudden revelations tonight."

Portman drove on for some moments in silence. "If she's telling the truth, we're after an outsider." He pulled at his tie and loosened it. "That complicates matters, eh?"

"Thinking of your wife?" Phin asked suddenly.

"Eh? Why, no. As a matter of fact, I was thinking of Latimer's wife." When Phin did not reply, Portman turned his ham actor's face towards him. "You really don't know, do you? Well, well. I wondered why he didn't bring it up this evening."

"Bring what up?"

"The *fact*—since he's so fond of facts—that his wife spent some time in a mental hospital, a few years ago."

"Wait," said Phin, and turned away to smile. "This is getting more traditional by the minute. Already we have the 'surly servant' and here's the 'dangerous lunatic'. A classic country house murder so far. All we need is the jewel-thief butler, the embezzling secretary, and I suppose the brother who's been away in Canada."

"You may laugh, but—"

"Who's laughing? I'm completely frazzled and frustrated. So spare me the pointless gossip."

"If you insist. But this bit of gossip comes from a colleague of mine who acted in the case. You see, she stabbed Latimer, and damn near killed him."

"What, *her*? I can't believe it!"

Portman registered a smile of triumph. "Ask Latimer to show you his scar sometime."

CHAPTER ELEVEN

THE NEXT DAY was Saturday, and Phin was to spend the evening with the Latimers, celebrating the engagement of their daughter to Martin Hughes. He intended to spend the morning, however, in the company of some of the world's more distinguished detectives: Sherlock Holmes, Father Brown, C. Auguste Dupin and many others.

He had long professed that the best training for the mind of a real sleuth lay in contemplating the cases of such masters, to whom the most impenetrably murky mystery was as transparent as a magnifying glass. Besides, since all the Unravellers were students of detective fiction, any one of them turning murderer might be expected to model his crimes on his favourite bedtime reading. Thackeray Phin accordingly left the receiver off his phone, cleared a space at the dining table, and plunged into detective fantasies.

At intervals he paused to remind himself of other plans for the day: studying his notes on Danby's death, cleaning his flat, eating, and shopping for an engagement present for Brenda and Martin.

On the other hand, he knew his notes by heart already. He wasn't hungry. He wasn't at all sure that it was proper to give presents to engaged couples.

As for cleaning his flat, it was an impossible task. The living room alone would require the labour of an intelligent and sympathetic librarian to make it tidy: nearly every piece of furniture and most of the floor space was heaped with books and sheaves of notes. Even the juxtaposition of the heaps was important, forming a kind of impromptu filing system. Phin knew that he could go at once to the armchair by the window and find a modest stack of books on Celtic mythology; next to it would be Mallery's *Picture Writing of the American Indians,* together with Phin's unfinished article on petroglyphs. The study of cup-and-ring markings had of course led him into cryptanalysis, so the next pile naturally included *Manuale di crittografia* and heaps of decipherment failures. Under the window were books on forgery, next to a box of slides demonstrating natural examples: flower-imitating insects, insect-imitating flowers, bird-like butterflies and a blossom which shows the footprint of a bird. Phin no longer remembered his own original association of mimetic slides with the Cabbala (on one side) or even with the *Register of Clowns* (on the other), but he had not the ruthlessness to disturb the arrangement, even to get to his desk. The dining table was now becoming his work place.

By noon, he gave up on the adventures of fictional detectives and went back to the tangled tale of the Unravellers. Yet, even as he went over the list of colour clues once more, he sensed the imprint of fictional mystery upon the whole affair.

One of them must be behind it all. Who else would bother setting up seven inexplicable incidents, each associated with a rainbow hue? He made up two lists.

VICTIMS

Stokes......................feared "Green", died mysteriously.
Portman....................orange thrown through window.
Latimer.....................ripped-up Yellow Pages.
Hyde........................card marked with formula for indigo.
Fitch.......................blue paint on tomb.
Pharaoh....................flowers stolen (violets).
Danby.......................died after "red tide" incident.

PERPETRATORS?

"Green"....................social worker?
                       (Pharaoh's nephew does social work)
Orange.....................greengrocer? (Pharaoh's father was one)
Yellow.....................solicitor? (Portman)
Indigo.....................Chemist? (Latimer)

Blue........................Painter? (Hyde)
Violet......................???
Red.........................Spy??
                          (Stokes claimed to be a kind of spy?)

The lists made only the feeblest kind of sense. He decided to try free association:

"Colour . . . horse of a different colour . . . Red Rum . . . murder . . . the Major's cipher . . . Red conspiracy . . . red tide . . . Red Sea . . . Dead Sea . . . sea-horse . . . zee-horse, Z-shoe . . . for want of a shoe the horse was lost . . . *Riders to the Sea* . . . Irish writers . . . the Celtic tradition . . . shamrock green?"

At this point he remembered an obscure quotation and stopped to look it up in the Celtic *Dream of Rhonabwy*: "No one, neither bard nor story-teller, knows the Dream without a book—by reason of the number of colours that were on the horses . . ."

"Back to a horse of another colour!" he muttered aloud. "I'm no closer to the truth than poor old Major Stokes."

He consulted a reference book: "In 1853, Green(e) was the 17th commonest name in England and Wales." He reckoned the number of Greens in the London phone directory to be over two and a half thousand. "Plus, of course, the nine million or so who might call themselves Green as an alias. Right. Let's forget about Green and all the other colours, and concentrate on the two deaths."

The afternoon slipped by unnoticed, while he chased the same few facts over and over the pages of his notebook. By sundown, he was able to formulate a few unanswered questions:

Questions on the death of Edgar Stokes:
1. How did he break his fingernails without scratching the walls about him?
2. How could a possible killer know his address?
3. Was he killed to prevent his appearance at the reunion? If so, why? Who was afraid to meet him there?
4. How did the possible killer get to him?
5. Is there any connection between the possible killer and Green?

Questions on the death of Frank Danby:

1. Why was he a recluse, acting like "a gangster in hiding"?
2. Why wasn't he glad to see his old cronies?
3. Why should he sit scanning the sea through a telescope when there was nothing to be seen? Why, half an hour later, did he not go out to look at the sea when there was something quite unusual to be seen?
4. Why should a man of action like Danby not put up a fight against his killer?
5. Why was he so indifferent to the reunion as to leave the invitation unopened?
6. Why was his furniture all shoved back against the walls, as though he expected to stage a dance or a wild fight?
7. If Sheila told the truth, who could have killed him?

He sat back, peering at his notes in the gloom. "I'm beginning to feel like a Watson without any Holmes." As he got up to put on the light, he stumbled over a chair.

"Ow! Damn! 'The singular incident, my dear Watson. The singular incident of the dog-tired detective barking his shins in the night.' 'But Holmes, he did not bark his shins.' 'Indeed, that is the singular incident.' I—*wait*!"

He snapped on the light, and with it came another kind of illumination.

"Right! That dog made a hell of a noise when the policeman went in to fetch it out. So why was it so quiet earlier? No one knew the dog that well, if it belonged to a recluse. So there's no question of anyone hiding in the bedroom! But that—that means —of course, I could have deduced that anyway. The facts are all there. All I really need to know is whether Sheila lied or not. Because if she didn't, this really is a classic case. Better ring Miss Pharaoh."

He hung up the phone, and it immediately rang. Whoever it was must have been drunk, or calling from a defective phone-box in outer space. When Phin shouted "Hello! Hello!" over the pips he got back only a mechanical buzzing, and a weak voice that might have been Old Hodge muttering something inaudible. The rest was watery silence. It was his American publisher, asking when Phin was going to do another book for him. For over half an hour, he subjected Phin to a monologue about ongoing situations, quick throughput, feedback from reviewers but backlash from the bookstore front . . . until at last Phin found the formula for ending the conversation situation: "Al? I'll get back to you, Al."

He did not, in fact, even get back to phoning Miss Pharaoh, for now a new theory had come to him. It took him a few more hours to work out the details, but sometime after midnight, he was sure:

"It's all one game." One person had hunted down Stokes and Danby in exile, someone had murdered them, for no reason except to challenge detection. The perfect crime—and no doubt there would be more examples of it before the game was over.

Only one person he could think of liked a game of wits that much: Dorothea Pharaoh. It was she who had picked out Phin as an opponent in the first place. The challenge was clear: she would murder Stokes, then Danby, and then the other three Unravellers, one by one, until she was caught. Of course she had no intention of being caught—she was as set on this as on any little logic problem or chess game.

It all made sense. She hired Phin. She arranged for him to be watching the premises while Stokes was killed. She arranged for the little trip to the Sussex coast to see Danby. No doubt she arranged all the little colour-clue incidents to point out her plan —defining the Unravellers as her intended victims. And a mind like hers was certainly capable of committing two baffling crimes: Stokes, seemingly, was murdered by someone able to pass through solid walls. Danby—as he had just proved—was murdered by someone who could not only pass through walls, but remain utterly invisible!

He picked up the phone and dialled her number.

A strange voice said, "Miss Dorothea Pharaoh's residence. Who's calling, please?"

"Thackeray Phin. I don't suppose she's awake at this hour— I've only just noticed the time—but if . . ."

"Could you leave your number, Mr Phin? You'll be called back."

He gave his number and hung up. Five minutes later his doorbell rang. He opened it to two policemen.

"Mr Phin? I believe you made a phone call to Miss Dorothea Pharaoh, sir."

"Yes, I—"

"Mind coming with us, sir?"

"I guess not. Er—has anything happened to her?"

The policemen looked at one another.

"Now why should you think that, Mr Phin?"

CHAPTER TWELVE

THE LIGHTS WERE ON all over Miss Pharaoh's mansion. Out front were half a dozen assorted police cars and vans, and other unmarked but official-looking vehicles. The policemen who were setting up floodlights in the front garden told Phin's captors to mind the cable as they led him up the steps. At the front door and inside there were guards, seemingly at every door. Passing several of them, Phin was taken into a front drawing-room, where a man in plain clothes sat writing at a card table. He looked up

"Our late caller? Good. Good. Mr Finn, is it? Ef-eye-double-en?"

Phin spelled his name and gave his address.

"Good. Good. Sit down, Mr Phin. And explain."

"Explain what?" Phin sat down.

"Oh, anything at all. Such as why you should be phoning a rich old lady at, er—we log your call at 1.43."

"I said on the phone, I didn't realize the time until I was making the call."

"Absent-minded, are we?" The man hunched his shoulders a little, as though to make himself look larger. "Let's stop fencing, lad. You wanted to know if anyone had found her yet, didn't you?"

"Found whom?"

"Surely *you* know."

One of the uniformed men spoke up. "He asked if anything had happened to her, Sarge. On the way over."

"Did he?" The sergeant looked at his watch. "We're busy, Mr Phin. Suppose you just tell us how and why you did it, and we can all get on with it, eh?"

"Sergeant, I'll stop fencing if you will. I gather from the enormous number of policemen here that someone's been murdered, and I gather from your hints that it's Miss Pharaoh. Now, if you'll bear with me a minute, I'll explain what I know."

"Good. Good." The detective sergeant sat back and listened to Phin's story, making the occasional note. Finally he said:

"You say you've been at home all day, and that you failed to go to this party in the evening?"

"I forgot all about it. And I don't have an iron-clad alibi for the time of death."

"What time would that be?" asked the policeman quickly.

"Whatever time it was. I presume it was after Miss Pharaoh got back from the party."

"She didn't go to the party. Anyone see you at home this evening? Anyone phone you?"

"A New York publisher—but I'm not sure of the time."

"Write down his name and address for me. Then you can go home. We may want you—"

"—again, so don't leave town," Phin said with him. "I'm already not leaving town on account of two other murder investigations, Sergeant. So I'll be specially careful to keep myself available. But I wouldn't mind a word with Chief Inspector Gaylord, if he's around."

"Have you anything to add to what you've said here?"

"No, it's the other way around; I'm hoping he can tell me what's happened here."

"He can't and he won't. Still, hang on a moment."

The sergeant left the room, and a uniformed constable took up a parade-rest position in front of the door. For a few minutes, Phin was forced to look at Miss Pharaoh's roll-top desk in the corner, knowing he would not be allowed within ten feet of it. Then Gaylord swept in, dismissed the guard and dropped into a chair. He began to rub his eyes.

"You don't waste much time, do you, Phin? I'm still not caught up on my sleep from your last murder, you know. If you plan on killing the rest of this crazy mob, do me a favour: get them all at once, will you?"

"What happened?"

"Looks like the au pair did it again. At least we're having trouble pinning it on anyone else."

"Listen, don't you think Miss Taverner's been through enough in the past few days? Why not leave her alone?"

"Because she has form, she's under suspicion for another murder, she has a flimsy alibi, she was the last to see the deceased alive, and she found the body. If that's not enough, she's mentioned in the will." Gaylord yawned. "I suppose you want to see the—yes, you would. We can, er, make a quick 'confirming identification' upstairs."

He led Phin up the dark stairway to a lofty, panelled bedroom on the first floor. A mob of men was bustling about the room, sweeping up bits of dirt, photographing every dim corner, dusting the tall mahogany wardrobe for fingerprints, unreeling tape measures. Amidst all this activity the small, quiet figure on the floor seemed almost forgotten, a film extra who wouldn't be needed after all.

Miss Pharaoh wore an old-fashioned frilly nightdress. She lay face down, but there was no mistaking the small dumpy figure, the untidy white hair now darkened with a patch of dried blood. Phin took a quick look at the face before he began to feel sick.

"The doctor says, hit on the head with a blunt instrument, then strangled with a ligature. Neither weapon's about the house."

"What are the weapons?"

"The blunt instrument has an unusual shape, and the doctor thinks it's a golf club. A driver, if you know what that is."

"I don't. And the ligature?"

"Odd again. Like a strip of something stiff. Iron, maybe."

Phin turned away. "Mind if we go elsewhere?"

"Not at all. But I hope you noticed the spots like bruises on the back of her leg, Mr Amateur Sleuth."

"Not really." Phin lurched from the room and stood at the top of the stairs, leaning on the newel post. Chief Inspector Gaylord caught his arm to keep him from falling over the railing. Phin straightened up immediately.

"Sorry. You were saying something about bruises."

"The doctor says they're not bruises, but lividity spots—something to do with what happens to the blood after the heart stops, the way it settles and all. Anyway, the indications are, the body was tumbled about a bit, and of course we'd like to know why. Come downstairs again and I'll tell you exactly what happened."

On the stairs, a man with a suitcase passed them, and stopped Gaylord to whisper something to him.

"Did you, by God? In her fist? That's something, anyway."

When they were settled in the front drawing room again, Gaylord said, "We've one clue, anyway. She was clutching an old-fashioned shirt stud. I wonder who'll be missing a stud from his dress shirt this morning? Someone at this party, I expect."

He yawned, and the aquiline nose seemed to snap down like a beak fastening upon his fist. "Here what we have so far: Miss Pharaoh was here all day with her au pair. Martin Hughes was here, too, working in the garden. Apparently Miss Pharaoh intended to go to this do in the evening, but then, about four o'clock, she made a phone call. Directly, she changed her mind. Said she had a migraine or something, and told Martin not to expect her at the party. Then he left. She had a light tea and a bath around six o'clock, says the au pair, then went to her room and stayed there.

"Sheila Taverner, the au pair, has Saturday nights off, as a rule. What she does is, leaves her child with a woman next door, a Mrs Gordon."

"I'm surprised at that," said Phin. "I wouldn't have thought there'd be anyone living in a neighbourhood like this who baby-sits."

"Mrs Gordon is not the lady of the house, she's a lodger. About half the house is cut up into tiny flats and furnished rooms. Sheila Taverner usually leaves her child with Mrs Gordon, goes out, and collects her in the morning. She says she gave—Mia, is it?—Mia her tea at seven, took her over, and came back to get ready for her night out."

"Where was she going, by the way?"

"She has a boy friend in Kennington who takes her to the local club for a booze-up. Ordinarily Miss Pharaoh lets her take the car—the yellow mini out front. She says she asked for it as usual, but this time Miss Pharaoh made a condition. She wanted Sheila to let her know when she was ready to go, because she might want her to make a delivery on the way."

"What kind of delivery?"

"I'm getting to it. By nine o'clock, Sheila was ready, so she tapped on the door of Miss Pharaoh's bedroom. Miss Pharaoh opened the door and gave her an envelope to be delivered to Martin Hughes, at the Latimer house. She was to hand it to him personally."

"Strange. Was it a gift? A cheque?"

"Hughes says not. On the phone just now, he told me it was a peculiar kind of riddle or something—but we're fetching him over here with it now. We've phoned the Latimers, too, and they confirm it. I guess he showed it round and they all scratched their heads over it."

"Did Miss Pharaoh say anything when she handed over the note?"

"Only that Martin Hughes was to get it personally. Then she asked Sheila to make her a cup of cocoa and leave it on the table outside her door. And she said, 'While you're in the kitchen, check that the back door is bolted.' Sheila says she did all this, brought up the cocoa and left it, tapped on the door and called out that it was there. Then she left. She drove straight to the Latimer house, gave Martin the note, talked with the others for a minute, and then went to Kennington. We're asking the Kennington police to check everything at their end with the boy friend. According to Sheila, they were at the club till eleven, went to the boy friend's place for coffee, and then she drove home. She saw the light in Miss Pharaoh's room, and the untouched cup of cocoa outside her door. She became worried, went in and found her. We were called at 12.58 this morning."

Phin nodded. "So, on the face of it, Miss Pharaoh died between nine o'clock and one o'clock. Has the police surgeon narrowed it down at all?"

"Yes. He didn't want to, but I pressed him. Officially, he says she died before eleven o'clock, very probably."

"And unofficially?"

"He's sure she died before ten."

The sleuth made a note of it. "It should be routine police work, then. Find someone without an alibi for that hour, who benefits by her death."

"As I said, we already have: Sheila Taverner. She could easily have brought up the cocoa, battered her employer and strangled her, then gone out as if nothing had happened. She has to cross the river to get to Kennington, so it would be easy enough to throw the murder weapons off the bridge. We've found a will in that desk in the corner, giving Sheila Taverner fifty thousand pounds. The will says it's a copy of the will filed with her solicitors, so I think we can take it as genuine for the time being."

"Any other bequests, Chief?"

"Another fifty thousand to her good friend Leonard Latimer, and the rest of the estate, amounting to this house, a couple of other properties, and about two hundred thousand, goes to her nephew Martin Hughes."

Phin made another note, and grinned. "There's a pair of suspects, then. How are their alibis?"

"We'll see when Hughes gets here. But you're satisfied with our case otherwise?" Gaylord's tone was ironic. "We haven't slipped up anywhere?"

Phin took the question seriously. "Have you found out whether Sheila, or anyone else, kept a set of golf clubs here? If not, where did the murder weapon come from? Not the boy friend."

"Why not, Phin?"

"Because then he either lent them to her innocently, in which case he'll say so and give her away, or else he's in on it. But if he's in on it, why didn't he come over and do the murder, while she established her own alibi? Anyway, why use golf clubs belonging to either of them, when the house is full of convenient murder weapons? No, either the clubs belonged to someone else and were kept here in the house, or else the murderer brought one club with him, on purpose."

"Very neatly said." The policeman smiled. "But that's not all we have against her. There's a question of security. The back door was bolted, the windows have special locks, the front door has a good security lock. That leaves us with only the open window of the murder room, and we've found no evidence that anyone used that, either."

"Wait a minute, not so fast. What was that about the front door?"

"A registered lock. No locksmith is allowed to make a key for it without written permission from the owner's solicitor, and he must notify the police who is to hold the key. There are only two key-holders for this one: Miss Pharaoh and Sheila Taverner. And there's no use getting hypothetical about picking a lock like this—it takes an expert.

"No, as I said, there's the open window upstairs. Thirty-four feet from the ground, above a flower bed which hasn't been disturbed for days. The window sill has the usual dust on it, and no marks in that, either. So we can rule out cat-burglars, drainpipe specialists and all that. The murderer came in with a key."

The door opened and a uniformed constable put his head in. "Hughes is here, sir."

"About time. Show him in here, Evans, will you?"

Martin Hughes came in and stumbled to a chair. His usual air of cheerful endurance was gone, his square shoulders slumped, and his long face looked haggard and stunned.

"I can't believe this. It doesn't seem . . . It couldn't be a mistake, could it? Someone else or—"

"No sir, it's your aunt."

Martin rubbed the razor nicks on his jaw. "She was like a mother to me. My own parents died when I was quite young, and Aunt—Aunt Dorothea took me in and raised me as her own. I have no other family left, now. Oh, the Latimers have been good to me, but . . . Sorry, Inspector. How can I be of help to you?"

Gaylord said smoothly. "I'm sorry to intrude on your grief, Mr Hughes, but there are a number of points we'd like to clear up. First, do you have a key to this house?"

"What? No, not any more. Wasn't it a prowler, then?"

"We'll come to that. Do you mean you had a key and lost it, perhaps?"

"No, I mean I had a key a few months ago, before the locks were changed. There had been a few break-ins in the area, and I urged Aunt Dorothea to have a good lock installed. She wanted to give me a key to it, but I refused."

"Why was that, Mr Hughes?"

"I'm a builder. When I'm on the site, I'm always having to lend out my ring of keys to one of the men or another, to fetch things. So it isn't as though I have constant control over them. As you must know, building workers aren't all model citizens, and any one of them could pinch a key without my knowing.

"Besides, I didn't really need a key here; mostly I come here to tend the garden. But why are you interested in keys?"

"Just getting the picture. Now, would you mind describing for me your movements of last evening? From, say, the afternoon."

"*My* movements? Wait, you don't think—"

"Your movements. If you don't mind."

Martin shrugged. "If it'll help, I suppose I must. Let's see: I set out some rhododendrons in the front garden here this afternoon. I really should have been at the site, but I wanted to relax, before the party. Working with flowers, Inspector, is my way of relaxing. Then I left here—in a bit of a huff, now that I think of it. You see, Aunt Dorothea told me she didn't feel up to coming to the party. One of her headaches, she said. I said I thought the least she could do would be to put in an appearance, even for half an hour. Anyway she wouldn't, so I went home."

"What time was this?"

"I got home about five. Then I bathed and dressed—"

"Excuse me, but dressed how? Was this a dinner-jacket affair, or what?"

"Good God, no. I managed to make myself wear a suit and tie in deference to the Latimers' wishes, but they didn't really expect formality. That's odd, though: Mr Hyde showed up, not long before I left the party, and he was wearing a dinner jacket. I wondered why, but I didn't get a chance to talk to him before I left."

Gaylord looked interested. "Now about this note you say Sheila Taverner brought you . . ."

Martin brought it out of his coat pocket. "Here. I hope you can make sense of it, because I can't. One of Aunt Dorothea's little jokes, I imagine. She likes—*liked* puzzles and riddles."

Gaylord read the note, looked at the back, and dropped it on the card table in front of him. "Did Sheila have any explanation?"

"None. I think she was a bit irritated at having to go out of her way to deliver it. She said that my aunt had gone to bed with her headache, so I thought it best not to ring her."

"Yes, I see. Now I want you to try to remember who was at the party, when they arrived, and when they left. Starting with yourself, of course."

Martin gave it some thought. "I arrived at about eight, and stayed till eleven, when I noticed that Mrs Latimer was getting tired. You see, she'd already made a buffet supper, and then she kept bustling about in her usual manner, making drinks and snacks, fussing over everyone. That's because she doesn't play."

"Play?"

"Oh, I'm sorry. I haven't explained that we were playing backgammon most of the evening. It's Mr Latimer's latest craze, and one of his business associates was there, so . . . But let me start at the beginning."

"Please do. Take your time, Mr Hughes."

"Right. I arrived at eight, and I think nearly everyone was there. Mr and Mrs Latimer, Mr and Mrs Portman, Brenda, and a Mr Garve who works with Mr Latimer. John Elliott and Marian, his wife, arrived just after me. They're both old friends from Cambridge. About the only friends I had there, in fact, since I left after my first year. And that's everyone, I think.

"We had a few cocktails, and then the buffet. Then Sheila turned up, sometime after nine. She only stayed a few minutes. Then we simply sat and played backgammon for the rest of the evening."

"I see. And did anyone talk about the murder of Mr Danby at all?"

"No. Derek Portman started to bring it up once, but Mr

126

Latimer cut him short. He said we didn't want anything depressing to intrude on this 'happy occasion'."

Phin's eyes asked silent permission of the policeman, who nodded. Phin asked: "*Was* it a happy occasion?"

"Well, yes. Boring, but I guess happy. I've never cared for backgammon, but it was the Latimers' idea of a wild party, so I didn't mind too terribly." Martin sighed. "Now, does anyone mind if *I* ask a few questions?"

Gaylord said, "You want to ask why we're so interested in this party, I imagine. The answer is that everyone who seems to have the slightest reason for murdering your aunt also seems to have been at this party—at one time or another."

"Including me, I suppose."

"You, Mr Hughes?" Gaylord was overdoing the feigned surprise. "What would your reason be?"

"My aunt showed me her will, Inspector. I know I'm her principal heir, and she was rich. That's always a 'motive' to the police, isn't it?"

"I don't think we need detain you any longer, Mr Hughes. If you'll drop by at the station in the morning, we'll take your statement."

When Martin had left, Gaylord said, "I don't like that one. The fact that he's got a decent alibi makes me like him all the less. I'd like to work on that alibi."

Thackeray Phin closed his notebook. "I always thought policemen were supposed to be objective."

"Don't you believe it." Gaylord picked up the note and read it again. "I don't see it. What do you make of this?"

Dear Martin,

Here's a little logic problem that ought to keep everyone amused for a few minutes:

A judge and a model were about to race their bicycles, up a certain hill and back down. One betting man overheard some bookmakers discussing the odds:

"The judge can go one mile per hour faster uphill than the model."

"Yes, but she can go ten per cent faster downhill than he."

"No one knows how far it is up the hill, or their speeds."

"It doesn't make any difference. The race is a cert."

Hearing this, and knowing that bookies are always informed and truthful men, the betting man put his money on—whom?

Your devoted aunt,

DOROTHEA

"Phin, what's wrong? Are you laughing or crying?"

"Neither, thanks. I guess I'm a little shocked at seeing the mind of my late friend, still playing tricks on the living."

"Yes, yes, but what's the answer? What does this mean?"

Phin wiped his eyes. "The answer should be obvious. But believe me, it has no bearing on your case."

"I'll decide that for myself!"

"Then maybe you should work it out for yourself."

Gaylord sounded exasperated. "I haven't time for games, Phin. Tell me, or by God, I'll have you for withholding evidence."

Now Phin was laughing. "Put away the handcuffs, Chief. I'll explain. Then you'll know as little as I do."

CHAPTER THIRTEEN

"TEN PER CENT FASTER . . . one mile an hour . . ."
Gaylord sighed. "I never could do these tricky distance problems.
What's the answer, for God's sake? Who does the bloke bet
on?"

"The judge, of course. If she goes faster uphill and faster downhill, it stands to reason she'll beat the male model."

"The judge is a woman? I knew there was a catch to it!"

Phin said, "Not really. If the bookmakers are all truthful, the
race must be a certainty. But since they don't know the speeds
or the distance involved, there's only one way that that can be
true: the judge is a woman."

"A lot of help that'll be. Here I sat, playing kids' games, when
I ought to be investigating a murder. You were right: this little
puzzle is useless."

"I didn't say that. I said the *answer* was useless. I think the
puzzle itself may come in very handy in solving this case. Espec-
ally if we can find out why she sent it to her nephew."

"If you say so, Phin. I prefer having a long interview with
Mr Gervase Hyde, and counting the studs in his dress shirt.
Meanwhile, why don't you go home and play with logic puzzles?"

Phin glanced at the roll-top desk in the corner. "I'd rather stay
here and—"

"Piss off, Phin. You might call that a police order."

Reluctantly, Phin allowed himself to be shown out of the room
and to the front door. The path was blocked by a uniformed
constable talking to an old woman wearing a dressing gown and
curlers, and not wearing teeth. She peered at Phin for a second,
then pointed a claw in his direction.

"'At's him!" she shrieked. "'At's the man I saw coming out of this house!"

"Right!" bellowed the constable. With some relish, he grabbed Phin in a hammer lock and started to manhandle him back into the drawing room. Gaylord stood by, seeming to enjoy the sight.

"'Ere!" the woman shrilled. "Not him. *Him!*"

She was pointing the claw past Phin, at Chief Inspector Jeremiah Huxtable Gaylord.

He spoke through clenched teeth. "Release him, Constable. I think we'd better step inside and straighten this out."

Fifteen minutes later, Mrs Gordon had been made to understand her mistake.

"Well, he was short, like you," she said finally.

"Madame, I am above average height," Gaylord said. "Now suppose you tell us once more exactly what you did see."

"Well—" she smacked her gums—"as I said, Sheila brought over her little girl *Miria* like always. I puts the child to bed—she's good as gold, you know—and then I sets down by the window to have a look-out."

"A look-out?"

"I'm not nosy, mind. I just like to know what's going on. Lovely view from my window, you know. I see everybody what comes in and goes out of this place. Call me nosy if you like, but—"

"Yes, Mrs Gordon. What did you see, exactly?"

"It was getting darkish, so I was just about to give up and watch the telly. Then I sees *him*—this man—sneaking out of the house. I couldn't make out his face, see, he had a hat on. But he was short, like, and he was all dressed up in his bib and tucker."

Gaylord said, "Do you mean he wore a dinner jacket?"

"Dinner? Oh, I get you. Like a waiter—yes, that's it. He was all dressed up like a fancy waiter. Fancy bit for somebody, I thinks. So I keeps watching, and next minute, here comes Sheila. Bold as brass. I expect they must have done in poor old Miss Pharaoh together, her and the waiter."

"But you had no reason to be suspicious at the time?"

"No." She gave it thought. "But these waiters is always suspicious, ain't they? Foreigners, most of 'em. And he did sneak out on the sly, like. Carryin' a white shopping bag, too. Wouldn't be surprised if it was full of silver.

"I didn't know what to think. But then I couldn't watch no longer, 'cause it was time for my favourite on the telly. Richard Baker, reading the news. I do like his smile."

When the constable had led Mrs Gordon off in the direction of her home, Gaylord asked Phin:

"Believe her story, do you?"

"Yes, and what's more I have an idea what was in the bag."

Gaylord's eyebrows shot up. "Clairvoyant, are you?"

"Could be. Tell me, have you by any chance found a plaster impression of a footprint anywhere in the house?"

"No." Gaylord thought it over, then said, "Wait a minute. Someone stole a few flowers and left a footprint, isn't that what you told me? And she cast it in plaster?"

"That's right. And now it's missing."

"Damnedest motive I've ever heard. All right, we'll keep it in mind. The point is, our neighbour saw a man in a hat and dinner jacket, no coat, creep out of this place at about nine o'clock, just before the news. And we've found the stud from a dress shirt, clutched in a death grip by the victim. Adds up, doesn't it?"

Phin had a wild look in his eye. "Adds up? It doesn't add up at all, Chief. It's wrong, it's—it's backwards, it's a paradox. I mean, when you ask 'Was she killed by one of the suspects in Danby's murder', what's the answer? *Yes*. And then again, *No*."

"That'll do, Phin. Thanks for your help, but we'll handle this from here."

The afternoon sun streamed in through one of the Latimers' round windows. Dust motes danced in the light, inspiring Mrs Latimer to another round of cleaning.

"I just dusted this place this morning," she said to no one

in particular. "It gets so *filthy*. And that cat, dragging in dead birds and I don't know what . . ."

Phin set his cup on the miniature coffee table. "Thanks for the coffee, Mrs Latimer. I'm sorry to be so much trouble."

"Trouble? Oh, you're no trouble. It's that policeman, that Gaylord. This is the second time he's called in here today, with his muddy boots. And now he's in Leonard's study with Leonard, asking I don't know what kind of awful questions—just because that Pharaoh creature's dead. I suppose they think I—"

She broke off as a door with a frosted-glass porthole opened and the two men came in. Leonard Latimer, in a faded dressing gown, shuffled over to drop his weight on the tiny sofa. Chief Inspector Gaylord made a slow circuit of the room as though walking a beat, and ended up leaning against the mantel.

"Hullo Phin, nice of you to drop in. I hope Vera hasn't been telling you wild stories."

"Wild stories?" said Gaylord quickly. "About what, for instance?"

Mrs Latimer again seemed to speak to herself. "Leonard keeps saying I'm upset, but I'm not. I never liked that woman and I never shall. No use my pretending I ever had any use for her." She turned to her husband and shook a duster in his face. "And no use you pretending she didn't have designs on you!"

Gaylord straightened up. "I'd like to hear more about this, Mrs Latimer. Suppose I help you carry this tray into the kitchen, and you tell me all about it . . ."

When they'd gone, Latimer started rubbing his head, in the old despairing gesture. "I don't know. I just don't know. This is about the last straw."

"Mr Latimer, do you mind if I ask you a few questions? I know you've just been over all this with the police, but I've got a personal interest in asking. Miss Pharaoh was my friend."

"We'll all miss her, I can tell you that. Brenda's in her room now, pretending to read the Sunday papers. But I know she's crying." Latimer's sigh was ragged. "What can I tell you?"

"What happened here last night, for a start. What time did everyone arrive and leave?"

Latimer explained that all the guests, except Gervase Hyde, had arrived before half past eight and stayed till eleven. He was sure that no one had left the house in that time.

"In fact, no one left the room, practically speaking. Of course Vera was bustling back and forth to the kitchen, but the rest of us stayed at the tables."

"The tables?"

"We shifted all the furniture and set up a couple of card tables in here, for the backgammon. It was a bit of a squeeze, but we just got everybody in, with the two tables shoved together and some extra chairs from the dining room. Quite cosy, really."

"And no one left the room?"

"Well, only to go to the loo for a minute. I mean to say, no one went out of here and across London to Dorothea's place. Couldn't have done, because it's a twenty-minute drive each way, at least. I could swear no one left the room for more than five minutes."

Phin made a note. "But let's suppose for the sake of argument that someone did leave for an hour. How would they get out of here?"

"You know, that's almost exactly what this Gaylord asked me! You must know your job, eh? Well, there are only two ways out. The front door here, which we could all see all the time, and the back door in the kitchen." He nodded towards the archway to the dining room through which Mrs Latimer and Gaylord had gone. "I'll tell you something else: no one but Vera set foot in that part of the house all evening. She wouldn't stand for it, you see, anyone messing about in *her* kitchen."

"Then that leaves the loo. Could I have a look at it?"

"Right this way." Latimer heaved himself to his feet and shuffled out, leading the way through the porthole door and down to the end of a passage. "Believe me, there's no way out of here," he said, opening a door.

"So I see." Phin drew out a magnifying glass as he stepped to the bathroom window. "Painted shut, all right. But what about this door?"

"My study, where I go when I can't stand Vera's eternal

133

house-cleaning. No windows, because you see it used to be a laundry room."

Phin indicated two doors halfway along the passage, facing each other. "And these? Bedrooms?"

"No, the bedrooms are on the other side of the house, beyond the dining room. As far as they can be from the bathroom, alas. No, these are . . . Well, this one is an old outside door. I think the idea was it would lead to the garage, only they never built the garage. Goes to the side of the house."

"Does it indeed?" The magnifying glass came into play again.

"Wasting your time, we never use it. I doubt whether we could get it open any more."

Phin sighed. "So I see, painted shut again. And the lock is caked with rust inside." He looked down at a small hinged flap at the bottom of the door. "I don't suppose anybody but your cat could get out through that."

Latimer chuckled. "Magwitch? Trouble is, he doesn't get out, he keeps getting in. I've been meaning for ages to nail the damn thing shut, he's getting to be a nuisance. Drives Vera barm—upsets her."

Phin turned and opened the door opposite. It was a cupboard, and after a glimpse of umbrellas and heaped shoes, Phin closed it. "No way out there. It's beginning to look as you say, that no one left the house by this route."

He allowed Latimer to lead him back to the lounge. "Yet I can't help but wonder . . . Practically everyone who could qualify as a suspect must have been here."

"Well if you ask me, it has to be Sheila Taverner or Gervase Hyde. I can tell the police suspect Hyde, just by the kind of questions they asked me."

"Oh? I wonder what they know that I don't." Phin polished the magnifier and put it away. "When did he get here?"

"Half past ten, quarter to eleven. Hyde's pretty damn unpredictable, you know. We had invited him, of course, but he'd turned us down. Said he had some sort of previous engagement. So I don't mind telling you it was a bolt from the blue when he turned up like that—late, drunk and dishevelled."

"He was wearing a dinner jacket?"

"That's what the police asked me. Wanted me to tell them if all his shirt studs were in place, but who notices a thing like that? No, I just meant his hair was messed up and he looked—you know, drunk. I think he'd had a violent disagreement with a taxi driver about the fare."

"What about his previous engagement?"

"He said, 'I've been stood up! At my age—stood bloody up!' Kept asking for a drink. I suggested he eat something instead, and he said, 'It's my soul that needs nourishment, not my belly. Come fill the cup!' I needn't tell you the little woman didn't care much for that kind of talk. It was after midnight by the time I managed to get rid of him. Had to drive him home myself, he wouldn't take a taxi again."

Chief Inspector Gaylord came in from the dining room. "I'd like to ask you about that myself, Mr Latimer."

"You already have."

"I know, but I'd like to get all the details straight. You drove Mr Hyde to his house, and then?"

"Then nothing. I left him and came home."

"You left him where? On the pavement? Did you see him go into his house?"

"No, but . . . What is this? He's not—he's all right, isn't he?"

Gaylord sat down and produced one of his slow, unpleasant half-smiles. "I'm afraid we can't find a trace of him. The young lady he lives with says he didn't come home at all!"

"Oh my God!" Latimer started rubbing his head again, as though trying to wear away the little hair remaining. "If he's—"

"If he's what, Mr Latimer?"

"If he's dead, that means someone really is after all of us!"

Gaylord said, "Oh now, calm yourself, Mr Latimer. I'm sure it's not that bad. Perhaps we'd better talk about something else. Tell me, are you a golfing man?"

"Eh?" Latimer looked up through his fingers. "Why yes, as I told you before, I used to play a few rounds. Haven't played for years."

"Keep a set of clubs, do you?"

"Yes. But I don't know where they've got to. Probably in the loft. Do you play?"

Gaylord shrugged. "Now and again." He looked at his watch. "I must be going now. Oh, may I use your facilities first?"

"Of course. Just by the study, you know the way."

"Thank you."

Gaylord vanished through the porthole door. Latimer looked at the sleuth. "He suspects me, doesn't he? My God, if Hyde turns up dead!"

"I'm sure he doesn't know whom to suspect," said Phin soothingly. "Hyde's rather suspect himself, I'd say. Tell me, do you have any other outdoor hobbies?"

"Me? No, I'm no sportsman. As you can see by looking at me."

"Every try ballooning? I hear it's getting to be quite a craze."

"Ballooning? You know, it's funny, but someone was talking about ballooning last night. Now let me think. Portman, it was. Said something about joining a balloon club."

"Did he indeed?" Phin made a note, and became aware that Latimer was staring at his notebook. "Oh, it's probably not important, just an idea. What I meant to ask you, about last night, was about the note Sheila Taverner delivered."

"That? I must say it was a bolt from the blue. I mean, I know how fond Dorothea is—was—of little logic puzzles and all, but it didn't seem quite appropriate."

"And what did Miss Taverner do while she was here?"

"Let's see: I was just coming out of the loo when she got here. Brenda answered the door, and there was Sheila with this envelope. She said she had a message to deliver to Martin from his aunt. The little woman wanted to give her a glass of punch, but Sheila said she couldn't stay a minute, and anyway she was afraid the police might stop her somewhere and breathalyse her. So she gave Martin the note and finally agreed to sit down and have some cake.

"Martin opened the note and read it, and he said, 'Is this all? Sheila, I can't make head or tail of it.' And he threw it on the

136

table for the rest of us to read. I said it seemed a bit thoughtless to send the girl miles out of her way to deliver a thing like that.

"Martin was all for ringing Dorothea to see what was up, but Sheila said best not to, she'd gone to bed with her headache and wouldn't appreciate having to go downstairs to answer the phone."

"Did Sheila act strangely at all?"

"I don't think so. She didn't finish her cake, but then she hadn't wanted any in the first place; Vera forced it on her. She waited till Vera was in the loo and then made a quick escape. Speaking of the loo, what's keeping . . .?"

"Right here, Mr Latimer." Gaylord came through the porthole door dragging a set of golf clubs. "I opened a cupboard door *by mistake* and found these. They're yours? I hope you don't mind my bringing them out for a better look."

"No, I—yes, they're mine. Look at the dust all over them." He started to reach towards them and Gaylord moved them away.

"Rather you wouldn't touch any of them just yet. Yes, I was just noticing the dust. And the odd thing is, one of them isn't dusty at all, is it? Wiped clean. See? This driver here." Gaylord seemed to be enjoying the revelation. "Just about the type of club we think Miss Pharaoh was stunned with, before she was strangled. I wonder if the killer tried to wipe blood from that club."

"I don't know what you're talking about."

"Very foolish, trying to wipe off blood. You see, we now have very sophisticated tests. We need only the tiniest trace of blood. An invisibly tiny drop is all we need."

Latimer struggled to stand up, then sagged back. "I—I'm sure that club's not mine. It must have been planted there."

"Really? But there's no other driver in the bag. Can't play a decent game of golf without one."

"I—I—"

"Better get dressed, Mr Latimer. I'm going to take these clubs to the Yard, and I think you might come along too. Just a few questions we'd like to clear up."

Phin sat stunned to silence until Latimer had left the room. Finally he managed to say, "Chief, you're wrong."

"Wrong? I haven't said anything."

"But I know what you're thinking. I knew it as soon as you started asking about his golf game. Then when you pretended to have to go to the loo . . ."

"Pretended?"

"I'll bet you never go while on duty—or any other time. No, you were looking for that club, because it fits your theory. And I'm telling you, your theory's wrong."

"What is my theory, then?"

"You think Hyde and Latimer conspired to murder Miss Pharaoh. Hyde brought the club here. Then Latimer killed him and hid his body. Isn't that about it?"

Gaylord feigned surprise. "Never crossed my mind. But we have started a search for Hyde's body, just in case."

"And the note? How does that fit your theory?"

"It's irrelevant. An old lady's whim."

Phin shook his head. "You thought the idea that Stokes was murdered was an old lady's whim too, as I recall. Don't you see what's happening? This is no ordinary murder case, with obvious clues lying all over the place. This is something planned, something devious—"

He could say no more, because Latimer came in. Brenda followed. Her face was tear-streaked, and she trailed a section of a Sunday paper as though unaware of what she was doing. But her words were sensible:

"Dad, shall I call our solicitor?"

Gaylord said pleasantly, "Oh, it needn't come to that, Miss. Just a few questions."

When the two men had left, she turned to Phin. "I overheard part of it. Dad's in trouble, isn't he?"

"Not yet. I don't think he needs his solicitor yet, but he looks like he should be seeing his doctor."

She sat down and propped the paper. "Aunt Dorothea's death has hit him hard. He's worried about his job anyway, and this is just one more worry."

After a moment, Phin said, "Look, maybe you could tell me something that would help him. Mr Hyde, now, did you see him arrive last night?"

"We all did. What do you want to know about it?"

"How was he dressed? A long coat or what?"

"A cape." Her face brightened. "Oh, I see! You're thinking he smuggled in that incriminating golf club? Wouldn't that clear Dad? Well, he could easily have brought it in under that cape. And the first thing he did was go to the loo."

Phin didn't know how to tell her this was no help to her father at all. "Er—what else? Did he look as though he'd been struggling with someone?"

"Yes. He said he'd fought with a taxi driver."

"Did you happen to notice his shirt studs?"

She thought for a moment. "You know, I don't think he was wearing that kind of shirt. I think it was a plain shirt with buttons. I could be wrong. One thing I did notice, his shoes were untied. Mum noticed it too—she always looks at everybody's shoes to see if they have any mud on them."

Phin said, "All right. Let's assume that golf club *is* a murder weapon. And let's say someone other than Hyde brought it back here. That means it's someone who went into that passage after nine o'clock last night, up to this afternoon. Who would that include?"

"Practically everybody. But I suppose you mean people who arrived here after nine—that means just Mr Hyde, and you and the police. And Dad, when he came back."

"So, in other words, only your father or Mr Hyde could have brought that club here after the murder."

She nodded. "It looks bad for Dad, doesn't it?"

"Not necessarily. Suppose the murderer had an accomplice. Someone brings the club to the house and—shoves it in through that cat door in the passage. And someone on the inside puts it away."

"You mean *Sheila*?"

"I know I'm grasping at straws, but tell me: about the time she arrived, who went in there?"

Brenda shrugged. "Who would conspire with Sheila anyway? Let's see: Dad was just coming out when she arrived. And then—" Her eyes widened for a second, then she shrugged again. "This is silly. It can't possibly have happened that way, so why waste time—"

"Look, if it's not important, why not tell me?"

She leapt up, shredding the newspaper as she turned on her heel to stalk out of the room. At the door she stopped. "All right, if you must know. It was Martin. Martin! Is he your murderer?"

To himself, alone with the miniature furniture, Phin said, "I wish I knew."

CHAPTER FOURTEEN

A FAT GIRL walking barefoot in the grass, gathering flowers—
that was the composition, worthy of a Dutch genre painter. Phin
paused for a moment, watching over the top of the low hedge,
before he raised his cane and waved.

"Good morning, Miss Taverner!"

"Oh, it's you. Morning." Sheila Taverner waved back with an
armless doll. She was gathering not flowers but toys. She was
not barefoot. And her flower basket was really a bucket made of
orange plastic. Seeing the bloom of health in her face, Phin had
built up the whole composition out of nothing.

He walked to the gate and put himself in the picture. "How
are you feeling this morning? Better?"

"I guess so. The doctor gave me some tablets . . ." Now he
noticed her listless movements, her swollen eyelids.

"Here, let me help you." Phin gathered up a stringless yo-yo
and a fire engine and added them to the collection.

"Thank you. I just can't seem to keep up with Mia. She's
always getting out her toys and scattering them. And I specially
want everything to look nice today."

"Expecting visitors?"

"Martin's coming over to sort through some of Miss Pharaoh's
belongings. This is his house now, and I don't want him to see it
messy. He—he shouts a lot."

"Does he? Why?" Phin found a doll's arm.

"I don't know. I guess I'm slow. Miss Pharaoh used to get
angry with me sometimes too. But Martin's worse. The slightest
thing upsets him."

"Are you going to work for him, then?"

"I don't know. I think he's going to sack me and sell this house." She sighed. "I just don't know what Mia and I are going to do."

"But I thought Miss Pharaoh provided for you in her will."

Sheila sighed again. "Not really. The money all goes into a what-you-call-it, a truss. For Mia."

"A trust?"

"Right. Mia gets it all on her twenty-first birthday. We can't get a penny before."

"Not even the interest?"

Sheila looked puzzled. "I don't know anything about that. All I know is, we don't get a penny until she's twenty-one. I read it in the will. It's in her desk."

"Mind if I have a look at it? I'm no lawyer, but that doesn't sound right. Miss Pharaoh surely didn't want you and Mia to go hungry for some fifteen years."

"Have a look for yourself." She conducted him inside, into the front room and to the old roll-top desk in the corner. Phin seated himself at the desk. Sheila Taverner took the will from a drawer and laid it before him. "See if you can make anything of it. *I* can't, I'm sure."

He read the document. "Are you sure Miss Pharaoh didn't explain this to you?"

"No."

"And you haven't actually seen her solicitor about it?"

"No."

"Then you'd better see him, at once. I think you'll find, when all the legal gobbledegook is translated into English, that you're entitled to the interest on fifty thousand pounds." Since she seemed to register no pleasure at the news, he added: "That means something like three thousand a year."

"Oh? That much?" Slowly it seemed to sink it. She grinned. "That much? Mr Phin, are you sure?"

"Yes, quite sure. Er—as long as I'm here, do you mind if I have a quick look through these other papers?"

"I don't know about that. Martin—"

"Mr Hughes won't mind, I'm sure. Naturally he'd want me to do anything to catch his aunt's murderer."

"All right, then. Would you like some tea?"

"Thanks."

He began with the pigeon-holes, all of which seemed to contain nothing but bills. In the drawers he found ledgers, cheque books, a tin box full of postal chess cards, a cardboard wallet stuffed with half-finished logic problems. A memo pad from the top drawer looked more promising: holding it to the light he could see faint impressions. Sheila brought in the tea while he was shading the pad lightly with a soft pencil.

"I've always wanted to do this," he said. "Never had the chance before. It says . . . Oh."

"What?"

"It says 'Marmalade, inst coffee, 3 lamb ch, fr asparag, kitch towels.' Not very helpful."

"What is it you're looking for, Mr Phin?"

"I thought Miss Pharaoh might have kept notes on the cases of Stokes and Danby."

"Oh, those. The police took some stuff away. Notes and things."

"That's what I was afraid of. Oh well, no harm in looking. Phin started rummaging through the waste-paper basket.

"Here's your cuppa tea. Just shout if you want a sandwich or anything."

In the waste-paper basket he found a rough draft of the note sent to Martin (with the answer checked) and a dry-cleaning bill. He then began pulling out the drawers and feeling behind them. When he was down on his knees, with one arm into the desk up to his elbow, a childish voice said:

"Hello, man. You look funny."

"Hello, Mia."

She squatted to peer into the dark recess. "What are you looking for?"

"My ears. I'm sure I left them here somewhere. Have you seen them?"

"Hee hee, they're on your head!" Something cold poked him

143

in the ear. He looked back to see the threatening end of a technicolour ice lolly, about to make another lunge at him. He ducked.

"These aren't my ears, I just borrowed them. My real ears are in the desk somewhere."

"*Not.*" She thought it over. "Miss Pharaoh hide them?"

"Maybe."

"She hided her box of stamps from me, but I found them."

He stopped searching and looked at the child. "Where did Miss Pharaoh hide the stamps, Mia?"

She pointed the dripping ice lolly at the upper part of the desk. "They come out when you pull that door down."

Thackery Phin ground his teeth. "I might have known. The one place I didn't look." He pulled at the roll-top, and as it came down, a thin box tumbled free, spilling stamps. Phin hardly looked at it; he was staring instead at a piece of note paper pinned to the roll-top, bearing words in Miss Pharaoh's firm hand:

FOOTNOTES

1. Frank's —— wading?
2. Gervase's —— meet at j.r.
3. Leonard's —— the "Edom" plan (PS 60 8) using note to M., alice-door.
4. Derek's —— sauna??

Item 1 had been crossed out. Phin could make no sense of the rest of it, and even the heading seemed peculiar: footnotes to what?

Then he realized the child was chattering to him:

"I can hide things too. I can hide Mia," she said. "I hided in that house by the sea and Mummy couldn't find me."

All at once he realized what she was trying to tell him.

"You did? Where were you hiding, Mia?"

"In the kitchen. I hided under the table. Mummy came in and didn't see me. Then she went outside again and cried, because she thought she was all alone."

Phin tried to keep his voice casual. "Did you hear anything while you were hiding?"

"Yes." She began licking stamps and sticking them carefully on the wall.

"What did you hear?"

"The man said, 'Who are you?' and then he made the funny noise: GAAAAAAAAH!" She giggled.

"And did Mummy hear the noise too?"

"Yes, and she ran out of the door. And then she cried because—"

"I see, yes. And where was Mummy when the man made this funny noise?"

"She was standing right by me. And she couldn't see me because I was under the table. And then the man made the noise and then—"

Sheila came in. "What are you doing in here? Take that lolly out in the kitchen this instant!" she made a swipe at Mia, but the child ducked easily and danced into the hall. "I'm sorry if she's been a nuisance, Mr Phin."

"On the contrary, she's been very helpful. We've just been talking about the other day in Sussex. When you were searching for her in Danby's kitchen, did you ever find out where she was hiding?"

"What?" She looked blank. "Well, no, but I found her in the road outside."

"She's just told me she was hiding in Danby's kitchen, under the table."

"What? But—"

"That's right, she seems to have heard *everything*. I think you'll be glad to know that puts you in the clear of Danby's murder."

"Whew! That's something, anyway. Only now I'm afraid the police suspect me of *this* murder." She stood chewing her lip for a few seconds. "I mean, they're always going to pick on me, aren't they? Because of my record."

"I hope not. I must admit, I didn't exactly take to your story about overhearing Danby's murder, at first. I thought it was strange, your being able to hear every word Danby said from the next room with the door closed. But now Mia has convinced me." He brought from his pocket a carved meerschaum and began to chew its amber stem reflectively. "I suppose the kitchen door was rather thin. And the hatch doors were nothing but thin plywood. Hmm. You must have heard virtually every sound in that room."

Suddenly he put away the pipe and stood up. "Come with me, I want to try an experiment."

He led the way to the morning room at the back of the house, rapped on its flagstone floor with his cane, and examined its thick oak door.

"This'll have to do. Sheila, you stay in the hall and listen. I'm going to walk across the floor in here twice. I want you to tell me which time I sound most like the stranger you heard."

Sheila listened close to the door. The first set of footsteps were nothing like those she'd heard, she explained. They were slow and kind of cloppy. Phin closed the door to try again.

"What's this?" said Martin Hughes. "Listening at doors, Sheila?"

"Shh," she whispered. "It's an experiment."

Phin opened the door. "How was that?"

"Better," she said. "Yes, definitely more like it."

"Hullo, Phin. What's all this? I thought Sheila was eavesdropping."

"No, we've just been testing different footsteps. Since practically all we know of the stranger who killed Danby is the sound of his or her feet—"

"Oh, I see. Have you heard the news? My future father-in-law's been released."

"I thought he might be."

Martin grinned. "You did? Mr Phin, if you know anything that can help him clear himself, I wish you'd tell his lawyer. From what I hear, he needs all the help he can get."

"I don't think I can clear him, exactly. I only meant I doubt if the police have a good case against him yet—or anyone."

Martin gave Sheila some house-cleaning instructions and sent her away, then he and Phin pulled up a pair of white wrought-iron chairs in the morning room and sat down.

"Brenda's worried too," said Martin. "And that worries me.

This whole thing was getting us down even before her father was . . . Anyway, I hope you'll continue sleuthing for me. I can't pay much, but—"

"Don't give it a thought," said Phin. "I've got a personal stake in this myself. By the way, I've just found this note of your aunt's, hidden in her desk. What do you make of it?"

Martin took the paper and studied it, while Phin studied him. With his thin, long-chinned face, his close-cropped hair, and his cheap, almost shabby business suit, Martin looked more than anything like an unhappy orphan grown up. And so he was.

"Greek to me. Can it be some sort of logic prob— No, of course not. With those names it must be somehow connected with the Unravellers." After a few seconds he added, "*Note to M.* That must mean the mysterious little note she sent me on Saturday night. But what about the rest of this—*j.r., Edom, wading, sauna* . . . What about this *alice-door*?"

"I think *alice-door* can be explained," said Phin. "We know your aunt was obsessed with word games and logic problems. She can hardly have been unfamiliar with the past master of those, Lewis Carroll."

"Oh, *Alice in Wonderland*, is it?"

"In which Alice encounters a miniature door only a few inches high. There is such a door at the Latimer house, the private entrance of their cat. Since Miss Pharaoh had a cat herself, I thought maybe this house too has an 'alice-door'."

Martin looked apologetic. "Nice theory, but it doesn't. You know, I've been over this house pretty thoroughly, what with all the repairs it's needed. I've never seen such a door."

Phin nodded. "Then she meant the one at the Latimers'. Oddly enough, Brenda and I were talking about that yesterday. There seems a possibility that some outside murderer passed his weapon in through that door, and some inside confederate put it away in the cupboard."

"Yes, so Brenda told me when she phoned me today. But then how would Aunt Dorothea know anything about that?"

"Exactly. She couldn't have been conspiring in her own murder," said Phin. "Maybe if I deciphered the rest of this note, we'd get a better idea. *Edom*, for example. It might be a misspelling of the cheese Edam, except that Miss Pharaoh never misspelt anything in her life, I'm sure."

"An anagram, perhaps?"

"That occurred to me. But all I can get is *mode*, *dome* and *demo*. Not very encouraging. And another thing peculiar here: notice that all the names are written as possessives? *Frank's* what? *Gervase's* what? I wish she'd been a bit clearer for once."

Martin thought for some moments. "It looks almost like senility, doesn't it? Secret codes—rather like the Major's crazy line of reasoning."

"Not a chance. Your aunt may have been fond of word play, but there's a big difference between this note and the insane ramblings of Major Stokes. No, this note means something specific. It's not like pseudo-ciphers based on *vodka*, or—"

Phin went quiet for a moment, and seemed almost to forget that he'd been speaking. Then: "Do you recall Mr Hyde's appearance on Saturday night?"

"How could anyone forget it? He was drunk and abusive, and he completely embarrassed the Latimers."

"Can you describe the way he was dressed?"

"Dinner dress. But don't ask me about shirt studs, because I just don't remember."

"How about his shoes? Do you remember whether they were tied or untied?"

After a pause, Martin said, "Untied, I think. Don't tell me *that's* important!"

"I wish I knew." Phin yawned. "I must admit I'm not exactly showing brilliance in solving these four deaths."

"Four? Is Hyde dead too?"

"No. I'm sorry, I keep listing the death of Major Stokes's cat as the first murder of the series. I blame this mysterious Green of his for everything."

Martin looked sceptical. "Surely not. Everything? Do you mean to tell me the same person butchered a cat, and then somehow killed Stokes, and then stabbed Mr Danby, and then strangled Aunt Dorothea? Not to mention all those mysterious burglaries."

"Green every time. I may be wrong, of course, but it does simplify things if I'm only looking for one murderer."

"But who, for heaven's sake, would do all those things?"

Phin showed empty hands. "That's the problem. Green never seems to stand still long enough to be identified. He's here, there and everywhere; he's one of the Unravellers but he's a total stranger; he has one motive for this murder and another motive for that—and no motive at all for Danby's murder, by the way. He has an accomplice, he has no accomplice; he kills without means in one case, without motive in another, and without opportunity in a third. He seems able to walk through walls—and what's more, he's completely invisible!"

CHAPTER FIFTEEN

THE GIRL WHO answered Hyde's door wore a kimono emblazoned with advertisements for obscure cigarette brands. She fluttered her single false eyelash in mock astonishment.

"You're *hours* too early, love. The party won't start till nine-ish, will it?"

"I don't know," said Phin. "Will it?"

"Come back nine-ishly." She started to close the door.

"Er—what's the party for, exactly?"

"It's a homecoming. For Gervase."

"I didn't know he was back."

She lowered the false eyelash and behind it took a closer look at this evidently stupid stranger. "He's not back, is he? I mean, if he was back, what would be the point of a homecoming? I mean, you don't have a rain dance after it starts pouring, do you?"

"I see. The party's supposed to bring him back. What if it doesn't?"

"We can always try again tomorrow night." She closed the door.

He spent the hours until nine at home, talking on the phone to the strangers who'd been at the Latimer house on Saturday night. Everyone told much the same story of Sheila and the mysterious note, Hyde's drunken arrival and the generally dull evening of backgammon.

At last he phoned Derek Portman.

"I don't know what I can tell you, Phin, if you've already talked to the others."

"This may sound strange, but what I'm really interested in is who went to the loo and when. You see, the police found a golf club in the Latimers' cupboard—in the passage to the loo—which could be the murder weapon. Someone had wiped it clean and put it away, possibly during the evening."

"Wait a minute—wiped it clean, you say? That's funny."

There was a pause. "Mr Portman? Are you there?"

"Yes, yes. Listen: I was thinking back to the time I went to the loo. I saw something that might be useful—but let's get our facts straight first. Where is this cupboard exactly?"

"Halfway down the passage, on the right-hand side as you come from the sitting room."

"I see. That's it, then. I opened the door—you know, the one with the porthole—and started along the passage. Mrs Latimer was standing there with the door of this cupboard open."

"What was she doing?"

"Just looking inside, or so I thought. But here's the funny part: she had a cloth in her hand. Looked like a damp cloth to me."

"Very observant, Mr Portman."

"It's all coming back to me as I think about it. I said, 'Excuse me, I didn't know anyone was in here.' She didn't say anything, she just slammed the door very quickly and rushed past me. I remember it well because she seemed upset about something. Of course by the time I'd gone to the loo and returned, I'd forgotten all about it. Now it seems important, doesn't it?"

"Thanks a lot, Mr Portman. Do you happen to remember where Sheila Taverner was at this time?"

"She'd just left. She'd only stayed five minutes. Seemed in quite a hurry."

When Phin, in dinner dress, parked his bicycle outside Hyde's house at nine o'clock, the party was already under way. The front door stood open, spilling out people, dim light, smoke and a hubbub of voices which all but smothered the beat of reggae from somewhere within. The entryway was choked with strangers trying to push through in both directions: a frail, worried-looking girl asking for "Fred"; half a dozen blond-bearded Australians each cradling a gallon of beer under his tattooed arm; the genial, tweedy editor of a quarterly review of what he explained was "Third World sci-fi". Phin pushed on until he found himself cornered by a Korean astrologer.

"Quite a party. You know Gervase?"

"Only through a couple of murders," said Phin. "He's not here by any chance, is he?"

"Couple of mergers? You're a businessman." The Korean held up a finger. "Don't tell me your birth date, let me guess. You can only be a Rat."

One of the Australians flexed his tattoo. "Who you calling a rat?"

"Forget it, Larry," said another, passing him a tin. "Keep an eye on the piss, while I find the bloody opener."

"Perhaps not a Rat," said the astrologer. "You may well be a Buffalo: authoritarian and traditionalist, you work for an old-established family firm. You're a Conservative. You hate to be thwarted in your ambitions. You . . . Excuse me, I think I see a friend."

Feeling suddenly conservative and headstrong, Phin bulled his way through the crowd into the next room, where a cheap wine (named after one of De Sade's heroines) was circulating, animating the conversation of a number of little groups. He moved through them, pausing to exchange words with this person and that: a witch, who claimed to be a reincarnation of Mother Shipton; a Belgian running an encounter therapy group for prospective diplomats; a prospective diplomat who thought that encounter groups were a waste of time unless they took account of what he called "the primal screams"; a country-and-western record producer "into" Krishna consciousness; an antique dealer "into" leather consciousness; a Cornish Nationalist poet. Crossing the room took Phin an hour.

"I know it's a failed movement," said the poet. "That's the whole point of it. Poets without a failing politics are even worse failures. Look about you. Those journalists—pathetic."

Phin followed his gaze towards a cluster of seedily dressed, overweight, chain-smoking men by the drinks table. They seemed to be engaged in the same furious argument they had been having an hour earlier.

One threw down his cigarette and ground it out on the carpet. "Economic viability, my arse."

"Pathetic," said the poet. "Notice how close they stay to the drink?"

A young woman stumbled into Phin. "Excuse me—Say, why are you got up as a waiter?"

Phin had heard the remark several times already. "It's not that," he said. "In a former incarnation, I believe I was a BBC radio announcer."

The woman herself was dressed, as were several others, in the costume of a Russian factory girl—but as translated by a Parisian fashion house. She laughed inordinately, asked him what he did, and when he claimed to be a private detective, laughed even harder.

"I'm a teacher," she said.

A journalist who had been weaving his way towards them now bore down on her. "A teacher!" he cried. "An educationist! Maybe you can explain something to me. Why is it you educationists find it important for our kids to make 'discoveries' in vital areas like guitar-plucking, and basket-weaving and rearing tadpoles, when they can't bloody read, spell, write or add two and two?"

Phin started drifting away as the woman said, "The ineducability of under-achievers has a functional correlation with the inoperative or non-integral family unit. Optimally, we'd like . . ."

Another journalist collared Phin by the door, as he was about to make his escape. "I heard you say you're a private eye. Why?"

"Because I am."

"You think Hyde's snuffed it too, don't you? Any angles on that?"

"I don't know what you mean."

There was a moment of diversion as two Australians, in a friendly tussle, crashed into a table in the next room.

"I mean," said the journalist, "I'm covering this Hyde business. His disappearance. I'd appreciate anything you could tell me. Are you working on this? Has someone hired you?"

"I was hired by the late Miss Dorothea Pharaoh to look into the death of a friend of hers. I imagine you've got that story already?"

"The murder club murders? That's the whole point, isn't it? Hyde must be number three—or is it number five? And do you think it'll stop here?"

Phin showed his empty hands. "Like you, I'm just waiting to see."

"Well, I hope something happens soon. We can't keep this story going forever, you know." The journalist was a plump man with thick glasses and scrofula. He introduced himself as Robbins of the *Herald*. "If you want my opinion, private eyes have had it. The divorce-law reform makes you lot redundant for that kind of work. The fuzz don't let you mess in their cases much. And all the real work's done by investigative reporters. So where does that leave you? Collecting debts?"

"I support myself by writing," Phin explained. "I'm not interested in debt-chasing or security. But you're right—the investigative reporter often has the time and the money behind him to dig deep, especially into organized crime."

"Very generous of you." The journalist seemed for some reason to want a disagreement. "I'll go further, however. The private eye is a complete dead dodo, an anachronism. Like pre-decimal currency, or fountain pens."

Phin, who used a fountain pen, blushed. "You may have something there too."

This stirred the journalist to further efforts. "I'll go so far as to say that the reporter has all the virtues of the old private detective, but none of the flaws. We're better observers, for a start. The old Sherlock Holmes days of guessing a man's profession by his appearance are gone—if they ever existed. The real point of observing is for identification, as the police well know. I could describe you perfectly right now." He closed his eyes. "Go ahead, try me."

"Describe me, then."

"American accent, six foot two in height, thin. Brown hair

parted on the right, blue eyes, large ears and a long nose. How'm I doing?"

"Fine." Phin covered his tie with one hand. "Can you describe my tie?"

"Black bow. Must be, since you're wearing a dinner jacket."

"That's not quite it. Everything you've said about my appearance so far is ordinary, I'm afraid. If you want to describe *me*, however, as I stand here, you ought to mention the extraordinary as well."

The journalist opened his eyes. "So I've missed something. Who looks at ties anyway?"

"Women do. So do other trained observers, like private detectives." Phin addressed an imaginary courtroom. "My lord, ladies and gentlemen of the jury, I submit that the witness's description could fit a hundred men in London. But he has failed to notice that the defendant was not wearing a tie!"

"No tie? Of course you're wearing a tie. I—Oh."

Phin lowered his hand. In place of a bow tie, he wore a large, purple-black butterfly. "The defence rests."

The journalist returned once more to his original point. "I still say investigative reporting does more good in a week than all the private eyes do in a year."

"Agreed."

"Organized crime, corruption, Thalidomide, Watergate . . ."

"Agreed."

"Just now my own paper has a team working on Rachmanism."

"On what?"

"Rachman was a landlord in the early sixties who used to buy up slum properties and extort higher rents from the tenants. He may be gone, but the same racket's still being worked in London. Only now the extortionists don't buy. They take over the management of property filled with sitting tenants—usually old people who have a low rent fixed by law. The landlords want them out, but they can't evict legally. So they hire a manager to do it for them. He comes in, winkles the tenants out, and collects a very large fee. If the tenants complain to the police, the landlord says he knows nothing about it. And if the police try to find the manager, he turns out to be a phoney name and a phoney address, with all payments made in cash."

Someone lurching past said, "Take the cash, that's my motto. And let the credibility gap."

Phin thanked the journalist and strolled away. Two Australians, wrestling playfully, slammed into him and shot him through a doorway. He collided with a man in anorak, jeans and muddy boots who was pouring a glass of wine.

"Hup, watch it—Oh, hullo, Phin. What brings you here?"

It was Gervase Hyde.

"I don't know," said Old Hodge, hanging up the phone. "Bleeder's either engaged or no answer . . . or else I lose the bloody tuppence like last time."

The publican looked sympathetic. "That's life, Old Hodge. Always an ill wind, blowin' nobody no good."

CHAPTER SIXTEEN

THE JOURNALIST ROBBINS was good, Phin had to admit. No sooner had he opened his mouth to speak to Hyde than the journalist glided up.

"You're Hyde, aren't you? The police are looking for you."

"The police? What's up?"

Robbins of the *Herald* spluttered. "Don't you read the papers?"

"Haven't lately, dear boy. I decided after my experience of Saturday night to get right away from civilization. No papers, no radio, no TV. Been down in Wales, at a cottage owned by a friend of mine, and I've been painting. I mean really working! Glorious country: clean air, clean food, and above all no boring bloody parties. I feel—renewed. You don't know how good it is to be where *camping* means merely putting up a tent, where sunrise is something to see, rather than something you've heard about, after you've been sleeping it off. Where—"

"Where the leek and the daffodil roam," the journalist said. "But just tell me this: what do you know about the death of Dorothea Pharaoh? Is that what you had to get away from?"

Hyde looked from him to Phin. "Is this a joke?"

"I'm afraid not," said Phin. "The police *are* looking for you. If I'm not mistaken, there are one or two plain-clothes men here tonight."

"Was she murdered?"

"Yes, on Saturday night. The night you left town."

"Oh God—poor Dorothea!"

Robbins said, "Kill her, did you? Or maybe you saw the whole thing. Doesn't matter, my paper wants an exclusive interview, and we'll pay. Need a good defence lawyer? You can write your own ticket, Hyde, as soon as I okay it with my editor."

"What? For God's sake, go away and leave me alone!"

"I'll be right back," promised the journalist. "Just as soon as I okay things with my editor."

When he'd gone, Phin said, "We won't have much time, and there are things I have to ask you. On Saturday evening—"

"I'd rather not talk about it. As I told the others, I had a date and I was stood up. That's all I have to say."

Phin said, "All right, then, I'll guess. My guess is you had a date with Dorothea Pharaoh. When she failed to show up, you sat there getting drunk on sake—"

"Did she tell you all this?"

"Of course not. She didn't stand you up at all, she was dead."

"But how did you know—even about the sake?"

"When you arrived at the Latimers', you were dressed for a dinner date. Miss Pharaoh left a note saying she was to meet you at a 'j.r.', obviously some kind of restaurant. Some of those at the Latimer house noticed your shoes were untied. From that I guessed it was a Japanese restaurant, the only kind which might require you to remove your shoes. Assuming that you waited there getting drunk, sake is the likely drink."

"Shrewd," said Hyde. "But 'j.r.' could stand for almost anything. How—"

"Some other time," Phin said. "I want to know what time you started drinking sake, and I want to know what happened after Latimer drove you home."

"I arrived at the Tanaka, the restaurant, at half past eight, and stayed a couple of hours. Is that an alibi, or what?"

"Yes. And what happened later?"

"Latimer drove me home, dropped me off, but somehow I just couldn't go inside. There was yet another bloody party going on here, and I couldn't face it. I just stood outside, and the longer I stood there, the sicker I felt. Sick of everything, you understand. I needed to get away. Then I saw a friend of mine coming out, Miriam Godolphin. I remembered she had this little cottage in Wales, so I asked her if I could use it. She took me back to her flat for the night, gave me a change of clothes, and I took the train early in the morning. I've been in Wales ever since. Just got back."

"One more thing: did Miss Pharaoh say why she wanted to meet you at a Japanese restaurant?"

"No, she—"

They were swept apart at that moment by a sudden surge of the crowd. Phin found himself crushed into a corner facing a woman dressed as a rich gypsy.

"I like the butterfly tie," she said. "Have you seen Clarissa?"

"Clarissa?"

"Lady Clarissa Venal. I'm afraid she's slipped off upstairs with her analyst."

"What's wrong with that?"

"You don't understand, she's got a thing about analysts. In fact, that's what her analyst is trying to cure her of."

Phin saw Chief Inspector Gaylord signalling to him from across the room. "Excuse me, I think I see someone I'm trying to avoid."

Before he could get away, Gaylord had worked his way over to him. "Phin, I've just had word Hyde's here."

"That's right, Chief. I was just talking to him."

"And you let him get away? Christ . . ." Gaylord signalled to two young men who'd been lounging by the door, and they moved off to block the exits. Both wore mail-order "sports clothes", and both had tied the sleeves of their jerseys round their necks.

The gipsy was interested. "I thought those two looked like fuzz," she said. "Who else would try to pass for Albert Camus these days?"

"Go away!" said Gaylord. He turned to Phin. "What did Hyde tell you?"

"He gave me his iron-clad alibi. That just about takes care of all your suspects, Chief. He was at a Japanese restaurant called Tanaka, all evening. And he's been in Wales ever since, and had no idea you wanted him."

"Never mind all that, where's the dinner jacket he wore that evening? I'd like to hear his story about the missing stud."

"I think you'll find those clothes at the flat of someone called Miriam Godolphin."

Gaylord made a note of the name. "Is that what he told you? It'll be a pleasure to check that one out." He cracked the half-smile, adding, "You see, Phin, we've already found those clothes."

"You have?" Phin was clearly impressed. "But where?"

"Here. In the dustbin outside the front door. It's one of the reasons we've had this place watched all day."

"Are you sure? Because—"

"Of course we're sure. Last night we got the girl who lives here, we got her story and compared it with Latimer's story. Now Latimer claims he drove Hyde home about midnight, dropped him off in front. The girl claims he never came in. Therefore, he must have begun fleeing then and there. And the first thing a fugitive does is get rid of distinctive clothes. I had the lads search the dustbins in front, and what did they come up with?"

"Garbage?"

"Have your laugh, Phin, while you can. They came up with a complete outfit: dinner jacket and trousers, old-fashioned boiled shirt and a boxed set of studs. The studs are exactly like the one we found in the victim's fist—and one is missing!"

"It's certainly evidence," said Phin. "But is it . . .?"

"Wait, there's more. We also found a hat. That remind you of anything?"

"Yes, the mysterious stranger Mrs Gordon saw leaving Miss Pharaoh's house."

"Right. And we also found—and this clinches it—a white plastic shopping bag, containing *a plaster impression of a footprint.*" Gaylord folded his arms. "What do you say to that?"

"I say you'd better check with this Miriam Godolphin anyway."

"You don't think we've found what we're looking for?"

Phin shook his head. "My guess is, the clothes you've found won't fit Mr Hyde. Indeed they won't fit any of your suspects, nor will the footprint impression."

"Phin, are you *still* trying to sell that mysterious stranger theory of yours? Because I'm not having any, thank you very much. We've got enough on Hyde to charge him now, once we find him. We know he was missing at the time of the murder. He was dressed like the person seen leaving the scene of the crime in a furtive manner, and we've got the evidence of the clothes, the shirt stud, and the footprint impression. He then went to the Latimer house, where we've found a possible weapon. And by the way, we've found traces of blood on that golf club. We know that Hyde then changed his clothes and ran off somewhere. How much more do we need?"

"You might need this. I found it this afternoon." Phin passed over Miss Pharaoh's note. "I'm afraid it's just as enigmatic as everything else she wrote, but I think it's evidence."

Gaylord scanned it and tucked it away. "Perhaps you'll be good enough to translate it for us sometime soon. Now if you'll excuse me, I've work to do."

One of the mail-order men came to report. "He's not upstairs, sir, but there's a sort of orgy—"

"Never mind that. Are the doors sealed off?"

"They were, sir, but P.-c. Parker had some trouble with a gang of Australians. It's possible Hyde got away in the confusion."

"That's all we need. Come on."

Phin trailed along after them to the front door. A row of police vehicles had drawn up in front, and he was just in time to see a pantomime horse being wrestled into the back of a Black Maria. Chief Inspector Gaylord conferred with the driver of a panda car for a full minute, then shook his head. "All right, then. Pack it in, lads."

Phin caught up with Gaylord as he was getting into his own car. "What is it, Chief? Has Hyde—?"

"Escaped? Not really. We just got a call from the local police station. Gervase Hyde has just walked in and volunteered information." The officer looked confused. "He must be bluffing."

"He's not bluffing. Hyde never carried a blood-stained golf club over to Latimer's house, for the simple reason that it was there already."

"Oh yes?"

"Listen. I've talked to everyone who was there, and I've got a list of the approximate times everyone went to the loo—went near that cupboard, in other words."

"Very useful, Phin, I'm sure. Drop it into the post to me sometime, will you? And now if you'll get your foot out of my car door . . ."

"But listen. The golf club could not have arrived before Sheila arrived, correct? Latimer was in the loo then. Martin Hughes went next, and then Mrs Latimer, and then Portman. But the thing is—"

"Another time, Phin. Good night." Gaylord nodded towards the house. "You may toddle on back to Sodom and Gomorrah, if you like." The door slammed and the Chief Inspector's car moved away. Phin stumbled on the kerb.

"Sodom and Gomorrah? Of course—*Edom* is another Biblical city. Then PS 60 8 probably means Psalm 60, verse 8." He dashed up the steps and plunged back into the mob, in search of a Bible.

CHAPTER SEVENTEEN

FITCH HOUSE was a huge, rambling barn of a place, part
Tudor, part Jacobean, the rest a mixture of messy additions. It
was said to have been a nunnery, closed down by Henry VIII
and turned over to a disreputable minor knight named Fitch, a
procurer. For four hundred years, the Fitches had resided here.

The Hon. Pamela Fitch-Portman directed her guests (the
three Latimers, the Taverners, mother and daughter, Martin
Hughes and Gervase Hyde) to a stretch of green sloping down to
a brook not far from the mansion. She explained the traditions
surrounding each landmark: the oak from which the Earl of
Cheniston hanged himself, the ugly iron sun dial, gift of the
Prince Regent, a stone bench called the Abbess's Seat, which . . .

Mrs Portman's shrill, refined accents floated back, as she led
them down a winding path to the picnic spot. She stood for a
moment on a little hill, raising her aristocratic profile against
the Magritte-blue sky, and perhaps sniffing the wind.

"We have a lovely day for it. That's right, just sit anywhere,
Derek and Mr Phin will be bringing the food directly."

Mrs Latimer looked up at the great house. "How do you manage
to keep it all clean?"

"How do we—oh yes, I see. Perhaps I ought to explain that
we no longer actually live at the House. Death duties, you see,
and taxes and maintenance made it impossible to hang on, as it
were. So we've moved into the gatekeeper's lodge—quite cosy,
really—and the house itself is let. Actually the Sheikh's been
quite sweet about it, allowing us to continue using the grounds.
Of course it's not the same but . . . hmm, yes. Well. Let's all
sit down, shall we? The food should be coming directly."

Grumbling like children, they sat down round the white picnic cloth. Empty plates and gleaming cutlery mocked them. The sun grew hotter, and somewhere a grasshopper started its metallic monody.

"There they are." Latimer pointed out two figures trudging over a near-by hill. "No, false alarm. It's that policeman."

Chief Inspector Gaylord and another detective came to take their places at the non-feast.

"I hope we're not disturbing you," said Gaylord. "Just thought we'd come to hear what Mr Phin has to say."

Hyde lay back, shading his eyes from the sun. "I suppose Mr Phin plans to 'reveal the name of the murderer'? I can't see any other reason for this unlikely congregation."

"I don't know his plans," said Gaylord. "But we're hoping he can clear up one or two points for us. Ah, here he comes now."

The others followed his gaze. From behind the gables and chimneys of Fitch House, a red and yellow balloon was rising. Slowly it grew larger, until they could make out Phin and Portman in the basket, waving their hats.

"I must apologize for Derek," said Mrs Portman. "Ballooning is his one childish craze. I so wish Mr Phin hadn't encouraged him today—Derek's really quite a responsible adult in many ways."

The balloon bumped down, narrowly missing the sun dial. Thackeray Phin, magnificent in an orchid-coloured pin-striped suit and panama, leapt out and helped tie it fast.

Latimer said, "Phin, was all this drama really necessary? If you just wanted to meet us, why—"

"Why make a meal of it?" Phin hoisted a picnic hamper from the basket, gave his walking stick a twirl, and said, "On the other hand, why not? I've no objection to sitting down to a picnic with a murderer, if no one else has. It's a nice day and . . . Wait till you see what we've brought."

Derek Portman brought champagne and Alsatian wine, to go with the summer banquet: tiny cucumber sandwiches, slices of sweet ham and succulent capon; chutney and pickle, salad and a fresh Coburg loaf; followed by jam tarts and cream scones, iced walnut cake and glazed cherry cake; both Indian and China tea; and of course shortbread.

For the next half-hour, the conversation lagged, as the adults set to it. Only Mia Taverner continued to refuse food, whining for an ice lolly. But when Phin finally explained to her, with all the authority of a television commercial, that the chicken was "real-chicken flavoured", she gave in gracefully and ate.

At last Phin folded his napkin. "Now then, on to murder. I think it'll help everyone's digestion if I unveil things slowly. Besides, we sleuths hate to give away everything at once. That's not the classic way, and this, I must say, is a classic case.

"First we have a murder which looks almost like natural death, and for which no one seems to have a motive. Then we have a set of seven mysterious clues, each associated with a colour of the rainbow. And these appear to lead our suspicions round and round, until they settle on Frank Danby.

"Naturally, as soon as we suspect him, he becomes our second victim. His death seems as pointless as the first—and even more difficult to have engineered. Consider:

"The murderer of Major Stokes somehow got at him inside an almost perfectly sealed house. The murderer of Frank Danby, on the other hand, got at him inside a house which was watched and guarded at every exit. What's more, the murderer could not have known just how thoroughly the house was guarded!

"More of these later. The point is, my own suspicions then fastened on the only one of the Seven Unravellers whom I believed capable of this kind of ingenuity: Miss Dorothea Pharaoh. Inevitably, she became the third victim. But here we have a twist on the locked- or guarded-house theme; this time, nearly every suspect worthy of our investigation was locked up in another house, miles away at the time of the crime!

"To cap it all, a certain 'mystery man' was seen leaving the house of Miss Pharaoh at about this time—and has never been seen since. Yes, this is surely a very Parthenon of a case."

Phin brought out his meerschaum and pretended to puff at it. He studied the faces before him, some bored, some expectant, some worried—one or two blank with fear.

He'd been watching them through the meal, noticing how characteristically they behaved, even in taking a glass of wine. Gervase Hyde, reclining on one denim-clad elbow, made a great show of "appreciation", testing the wine for colour, tasting it—but guzzling it thirstily. Derek Portman went through the same motions of testing, but mechanically. He was evidently uncomfortable at having to sit on the grass, staining his tennis whites and being unable to assume a striking pose. He barely tasted the wine, then set his glass aside until, as he probably thought, the script should call for him to take another sip.

Pamela Fitch-Portman made no fuss at all, of course. She had learned that trick of aristocratic women, of being a charming and well-groomed object when noticed, but otherwise blending into the background. Phin had to force himself to see her, the neat black hair shot with grey, the delicate small face sagging about the eyes, the long embroidered "Chinese" dress whose high collar nearly hid her incipient goitre.

Leonard Latimer used wine as something to wash down the enormous quantities of food he gathered in. The entire meal seemed for him an agony, for the little eyes in his fat cheeks kept darting about to see who was watching him eat. Between courses he fidgeted with his wine glass, threatening to break its stem.

Vera Latimer studied her wine glass before taking anything, and polished it with her serviette. Her daughter blotted her lipstick before accepting a glass of what she called "champers", which she kept trying to hold in a carelessly graceful manner until she succeeded in spilling it. Sheila grudgingly helped her clean it up.

Martin Hughes was uninterested in the wine. It was clear from the set of his long chin that he disapproved of the whole wasteful banquet. But he collected all the lead foil from the bottles and stuffed it into a side pocket of his baggy brown jacket.

Sheila Taverner seemed genuinely to enjoy the wine and the meal, growing quite flushed and almost animated. The company still made her feel an outsider, no doubt, for she kept glancing at the other women's clothes. Phin guessed she was comparing Mrs Portman's Chinese robe and Brenda's clean-looking summer dress of blue and white, with her own dull pink smock and blue jeans. But as she continued to drink, some of the heavy sullenness lifted from her plump face. Her black hair began to straggle out of the elastic band gripping it at the back of her neck. And finally she sat watching her child skip and tumble on the grass, watching with pleasure.

The successful solicitor, the failed painter, the au pair . . . Phin puffed at his empty pipe and considered them all again, his collection of psychological silhouettes. He took no pride in these portraits; some were incomplete, all were superficial; and one was certainly wrong. He was certain of two things: murderers do not go about betraying themselves through small unconscious actions. And one of the persons before him was certainly a murderer.

"A classic case. A Parthenon of a case," he said aloud. "Or is it? Is this case classical like the noble columns of the Parthenon? Or is it 'classical' like the façade of a bank in Kansas City—a cheap, false, *put-up job*?"

Latimer, who'd been tying knots in the corners of his handkerchief, looked up. "Fake, eh? You know, I had the same idea. Stokes could have faked his own death, and then—"

"Oh, I don't mean simply a fake death or two. I mean a complete false impression, built up carefully around three real murders." He paused, waiting for Latimer to put the improvised handkerchief cap over his bald spot, already pink from the sun. "Let's take those mysterious colour-clue incidents, for example:

"Why should anyone throw an orange through Portman's office window? Why leave Latimer a clue from the Yellow Pages? Why give Hyde a diagram of an indigo molecule, or put blue paint on the tomb of Sir Anthony Fitch, or steal violets from Miss Pharaoh's garden? And why drop red dye into the sea before Danby's house?

"I can think of two excellent reasons. One is, simply to dazzle. We are to be blinded with lying clues in the hope that we'll overlook the one genuine clue among them. G. K. Chesterton said it well enough: 'Where would a wise man hide a leaf? In a forest.'

In one of his stories, a black man hides—among blackface minstrels. And so, taking a leaf from Chesterton, we ask:

"Where does Green hide? In a rainbow."

After a significant pause, Hyde said, "I follow the metaphor, but not the exact application. You mean this Green person is in hiding, somehow?"

"Hiding under false colours, Mr Hyde. We know the orange and the indigo and the blue were nonsensical clues. We were led to believe that Green himself might be nonsense."

Portman said, "But Green *is* nonsense, isn't he? None of us knows anything about him, or has ever seen his face."

"One of us," Phin said, "may well see his face daily, in the mirror. Shaving? Or perhaps putting on make-up?"

Gaylord cleared his throat irritably.

"All right, Chief, I'll get on with it. Let's begin by listing what we know for sure about Green. He probably uttered threats against Major Stokes. He certainly broke into his house and smashed up his crockery, and he certainly murdered his cat. Over the past month or so, Green made quite a nuisance of himself.

"But until recently, Green was not a murderer. His threats and actions were not murderous, but harrassing. Indeed, he must have passed up a few chances, during his visits to Stokes, to murder him. He possibly had no intention of killing Stokes, until—"

"Until Dorothea announced the reunion," said Latimer. "That means it has something to do with the Unravellers. Just as I've always said."

"Yes, Green could not allow Stokes to attend that reunion. Can anyone think why?"

Brenda Latimer said, "To keep him from talking to the others?"

Martin frowned at her. "Don't be silly, darling. He did talk, didn't he? Talked on the phone to Aunt Dorothea. And he could have talked to anybody. Must be some other reason."

"There's one thing Stokes knew which he could have told the others," Phin said. "Which he could only have told them at the reunion, not on the phone."

"What's that, pray tell?" asked Portman.

Phin pointed to him. "Stokes could have looked among the faces present, and pointed to one, and said, 'That face! That's the face of Green!'"

Hyde said, "That won't wash, Phin. If one of us didn't want to be identified, he could easily have stayed away from the reunion. Why commit murder instead? This isn't logical."

"No?" Phin puffed for a moment at his empty pipe. "What if I were to tell you that there was one person *who could not stay away from the reunion? Who could not avoid being seen there by Major Stokes?*"

"I'd say there's no such person," said Hyde. "No one had to be there but Dorothea herself. And she could always call off the reunion. Anyway, I thought Green was a man."

Phin nodded. "Stokes thought so, but there's no reason why Green couldn't have been a woman impersonating a man."

"This is getting sillier and sillier," said Martin. "Look, I didn't have to be there, and as a matter of fact I wasn't planning on being anywhere near this absurd reunion. And I don't think you can pin this on Sheila, either."

Sheila said, "You think I had to be there? I didn't. In fact Miss Pharaoh said she was getting in outside caterers to handle everything."

Hyde brushed his moustache and beamed at Phin. "There. Your logic has defeated itself."

"Maybe. But let me carry on with my defeated logic for a minute more. Let's *assume* that someone here was using the name Green to mask his true identity, while he pursued certain activities. By pure chance, his activities came to the notice of Major Stokes—"

Brenda said, "Wait a minute. Are you saying this Green was some sort of spy or something? Or a Nazi war criminal?"

"No, a peace criminal of a fairly modern British type. The crime may seem petty enough, but then our criminal had a reputation to protect."

Portman said, "Stop beating about the bush and just tell us, what kind of criminal?"

Phin looked surprised. "I should have thought you of all people would have guessed. What kind of person would kill an old pensioner's cat, smash up his belongings, and offer him money to leave town? Who would offer this kind of 'harassment', who but a landlord?"

"I resent that." Portman adjusted his tie and sat up straight. "I happen to own property, and there's no law against my renting it."

"But some landlords are not so particular about the law, are they? The legal term for what they do is 'harassment', but the fact can amount to broken crockery or even broken arms. Some landlords even hire agents to do their dirty work for them."

"But not murder," said Portman, beginning to look amused.

"Not normally murder. But now, let us suppose *you* were Green. You're working away, busily digging old people out of their homes so that you can sell them for higher prices, and one of your tenants happens to be your old comrade, Stokes. Since he's senile, he no longer remembers you. You of course have no qualms about bullying him, since you've always hated his guts.

"Then you learn there is to be a reunion, and a chance that somehow Stokes will learn your true identity. You take the easy way out, and kill him."

"I do?" Portman chuckled. "Why, for heaven's sake?"

"You have everything to lose, as an upright, respectable solicitor, by being publicly exposed as Green. Your entire Jekyll –Hyde existence—oh, sorry, Mr Hyde—your elaborate hypocrisy is threatened, by one old man who's easy enough to kill."

"Easy, eh? All right, how do I go about it?"

"Since you'd ransacked the place earlier, you know all about the Major's collection of medicines: he has a weak heart and a weak bladder. At some time each evening he will go down to the toilet—the only room in his house which has an open window."

"You said it was too small," Portman reminded him.

"Too small for a man, but not for a murder weapon. What's the easiest weapon to use, for causing a weak old man to have heart failure?"

"I don't know—smothering with a pillow?"

"Exactly. But the pillow must be small enough to go through a tiny window, an air vent, really. Also it must be large enough to fill the little room he's in. It must seize him and hold him against the wall, while he struggles and claws and breaks his fingernails against it—and dies."

"Small but large," said Hyde mockingly. "It seems we have another paradox." Then he noticed where Phin was pointing insistently, with the amber stem of his pipe. "The balloon! *The damned balloon!*"

"It fits every criterion," said Phin. "Deflate it, shove it through the hole, and inflate it inside. And then it's made of tough plastic. You see, Stokes tore his nails clawing at something and yet there was nothing left *under* his nails. That rules out flesh or cloth or wood or paint or plaster—but it doesn't rule out the tough material of this balloon."

Portman looked sick. "God! I think—I think I need to call *my* solicitor."

Chief Inspector Gaylord flashed his look of kindly menace. "Oh, don't bother with that, sir. What's the point? After all, we're only having a friendly teet-à-teet, eh?"

After some minutes, Portman recovered most of his bravado. "Phin, you're skating dangerously close to slander, you know that? You'll never prove a thing about Stokes's death. As you describe it, it's a perfect crime. I'll go further." He leaned over to shake his finger at the sleuth. "It's *the* perfect crime. *If* I were Green, I'd have stopped there. Quit while I was winning."

Phin looked glum. "It is perfect, isn't it? I can prove motive easily enough, and even opportunity. It's the method I can't prove.

"And when we get to the murder of Frank Danby, I'm in more trouble. In this case, there's no clear motive. Not a single one of us who was there that day had the slightest reason to kill Danby."

"So Green was a stranger after all!" said Brenda.

"So it seems. Let's cast our minds back to that day. The cycle of mysterious colour-clues was almost complete, except that

171

Danby had not yet received his 'red' clue. Miss Pharaoh dragged us all down there to find out why.

"But Danby's behaviour was an even greater mystery. He kept insulting everyone, and hinting that he wanted to be alone. He hadn't even opened Miss Pharaoh's invitation, or any of his other post. He kept a savage guard dog. It was as though he were afraid of someone or something. A neighbour had noticed it, too. She said Danby acted like 'a gangster hiding out from the law', more than a retired security officer. *Why?*

"When we first saw him, he was scanning the sea with a telescope, yet there wasn't anything to see. Later, when we all ran out to look at the red dye in the water, he couldn't be bothered to leave his chair. Again, *why?*"

"He was already dead," said Martin.

"So I thought, at first. But it's not the answer, according to those who heard him die."

Mrs Latimer startled them all by speaking for the first time. "I know why he stayed in. He was planning to kill himself. Anyone living in a dirty pig sty of a house like that would have to end up a suicide, it stands to reason."

"He was murdered," Phin insisted. "By Green. Let's consider all the incidents in order. We all left and ran down to the beach. The last person to leave was either Miss Pharaoh or Miss Latimer."

"I was the last," said Brenda. "I ran back to put down the knife. I'm still confused about it but—I think I must have laid it on the hamper, in the centre of the room."

"It doesn't matter," said Phin generously. "Danby was still alive after you left, as we'll see. The next thing you, Mr Hyde, wandered up close to the house to get a perspective view of the stain in the water. You were there long enough to slip inside and do the job."

"But I didn't, my dear Phin."

"Apparently not. Because after you started back towards the beach, Sheila Taverner went round to the back of the house, and went inside, and heard the murder take place."

"So she says," Portman intruded.

"Yes, she says she was looking for her daughter Mia. She saw the back door standing open, and went in and heard the murder. And immediately ran out. What she didn't know at the time was, Mia was there, hiding under the kitchen table. So Mia heard the murder too."

"I can vouch for that," said Chief Inspector Gaylord. "Phin interrogated the child for me this morning. He wiggled his ears for her, and she came out with the whole story. Chilling detail, I might add."

Phin resumed: "Then Sheila ran outside, and Mia ran out after her, and rejoined her in the road. And then they heard you, Mr Latimer, calling out that Danby was dead.

"Those are the facts, to which we can add Danby's last words: 'Who the hell are you? What do you want?' "

" 'GAAAAAAAH'," Mia prompted, and Phin shuddered.

"Uh, thank you, Mia. The words imply that Danby did not recognize his killer. Yet he had just been introduced to every one of us there. So we surmise that Green was, in this, case, a total stranger, not of our group.

"But this makes another problem. At the moment of the murder, both the front and the back of the house were watched. Mia and Sheila were in the kitchen. Latimer and Martin must have been well on their way to the front door, and could not have failed to notice anyone coming out that way. So Green, having committed his bloody deed, had only one escape: he could go through the bedroom and out by a side window. But that exit too was blocked off by a dog. When a policeman went in to fetch the dog out later, it went off like a very efficient alarm. A frenzy of barking, as soon as anyone went into the bedroom. Why did we hear no such barking when Green went in?"

"That's an old Sherlock Holmes problem," said Latimer. "The answer is, Green and the dog knew each other."

"*Very* unlikely, but let's say it's true. Green gets past the dog and to the bedroom window. But the sill of that window is coated thickly with dust, and the police found no sign of disturbance. It's impossible for anyone to have climbed out of that window."

"In other words, *Green could only escape from that house by becoming invisible.*"

173

"I don't understand," said Brenda. "You're not suggesting—"

"No. I'm suggesting that Green, the mysterious stranger, never existed. No stranger killed Frank Danby. *It was one of us.*

"It was someone in our group, whom Danby had been introduced to a few minutes earlier. But whom he didn't recognize."

"A disguise!" Hyde shouted. "I'm beginning to like this!"

Phin looked helpless. "I've given you all every possible hint, and you still don't grasp it? Danby doesn't open his letters— why? He's not interested in going out to see the sea incarnadined —why? For the same reason he kept a clock with no crystal, and retired early from the security agency:

"Frank Danby was partially or totally blind."

After a few seconds, Martin said, "Wait a minute. We all saw him looking at the sea through a telescope."

"As I recall, Admiral Lord Nelson was once seen looking through a telescope," said Phin. "He saw nothing through it, however. The telescope incident should have told us, if nothing else."

Brenda said, "How do you mean?"

"Try using a telescope while wearing sunglasses sometime. Or any glasses. You won't see a thing, unless you bring the instrument closer to your eye. There was nothing to look at anyway—that was just a performance for our benefit.

"When a proud, tough, physical man like Danby goes blind, what would you expect him to do? Buy a tin cup and an accordion? Or go into hiding and lick his wounds? Blindness explains every part of his inexplicable behaviour. His rudeness, his reclusiveness, his unopened mail—he even kept his furniture shoved back against the walls, out of his way.

"Yes, blindness explains everything, and it's the simplest explanation. Moreover it explains the peculiar invisibility of Green.

"I said before that Martin and Mr Latimer were 'well on their way to the front door' at the time of the murder. Indeed, one of them was already through the front door and jabbing that bread knife into Danby's throat."

"Just a minute," said Latimer. "I want to—"

"Confess? It would be most helpful."

Later, all they could agree on was that Mrs Latimer had started the little riot, when she flung the milk jug at Phin's head. The rest wasn't clear at all: was it true she'd tried to follow it up with the pot of boiling tea? Was it Portman who restrained her, or Chief Inspector Gaylord? And who was it caught the fainting Mrs Portman, keeping her from falling face down in the jam tarts? And who kept Hyde from braining Latimer with a champagne bottle? Not Sheila, for she was trying to stop Mia trampling energetically on the plate of cream scones. Not Brenda, either, for she had fallen screaming into her father's arms.

One thing was clear, however. The person who finished off the riot by seizing the picnic cloth, whipping it up and throwing it over the lot of them—the person who then hurried to the balloon and cast off the mooring line—was Martin Hughes.

CHAPTER EIGHTEEN

THE FIRST THING Gaylord said when his head emerged from the cloth was, "Phin, I hold you completely responsible." He wiped thick cream from his ear, rummaged in his pocket and came up with a tiny radio. Then began an incomprehensible series of police messages:

"Bossa Nova to Rumba, Bossa Nova to Rumba . . . Put out a call to Cakewalk, Beguine and Bolero. Tell Polka, Can-Can and Hokey-Cokey to take up their positions and stand by . . . What we're chasing is a red and yellow balloon. Not saloon, *balloon* . . . B as in Big Apple . . . How do I know what the number is, I didn't even know they had numbers . . . Right, yes . . . Better call Polonaise or Schottische, ask them to put up a helicopter . . ."

"Rumba times your message at fifteen-fourteen . . ." said the radio.

But the eventual capture of Martin Hughes's get-away craft had nothing to do with such dance instructions. The wind was gradually shifting, carrying the red and yellow object back towards Fitch House. At one of the upper windows of the house appeared a friendly bearded face framed in a burnous.

"It's the Sheikh," said Portman. He removed his hat and waved it, then pointed at the balloon.

The Sheikh disappeared from the window. He reappeared a moment later, sighting along the barrel of a long Arab rifle.

"He can't do that!" said Gaylord.

The Sheikh had done it already. As a convoy of police cars (probably Charleston and Fandango) raced up the drive of Fitch House, the balloon descended slowly to meet them.

"I didn't want to be involved, and I didn't want Martin to be involved," Latimer explained. "It was all such a nightmare!"

"So you lied," said Phin.

"I half-lied. I said I *thought* Martin and I went into Danby's house together, but I couldn't be sure."

"I'm glad you've confessed, as I'm sure you are. Now let me see if I can reconstruct what really happened. Sheila heard the killer's footsteps. They weren't the slow, clopping footsteps of a man whose shoes are untied and half coming off. They weren't *your* footsteps, in other words."

"That's right." Latimer sat cradling both the women in his life, one arm round each. "What happened was this: just as we got to the front steps, one of my shoes came off. I sat down to shake the gravel out of it while Martin went on inside. He was only in there a few seconds. I—I just couldn't believe—"

"That I'd murder a perfect stranger?" said Martin. "I didn't." In the company of Gaylord and two uniformed constables, he approached the picnic site. The four of them sat down awkwardly, a short distance from the others.

"I've done nothing," Martin emphasized. "And I don't have to stay here."

"You've stolen a balloon," said Gaylord. "I've charged you with it, and you'll stay where I put you. I don't choose to miss the rest of Mr Phin's little lecture on your account, so stay put."

Brenda wiped her tears. "I'm sorry, Mr Phin, I just can't believe any of this. Just because Martin panicked doesn't mean he's your murderer."

"Bit puzzled myself," said Portman. "Martin's no balloonist, as we've just seen. Damn near hit the house. How do you propose to show he killed old Stokes?"

Phin shook his head. "Not with a balloon. Miss Latimer gave me a hint when she spoke of their trip to France. 'We never unpacked the boat,' she said. Could the boat have been an inflatable rubber dinghy? Bought at a military surplus place?"

"You're right," said Brenda. "How did you know?"

"I guessed. Those surplus air-sea rescue dinghies are perfect for the job—small enough to go through the window, and they quickly inflate to full size. And often they come with extras—such as red dye marker. It's characteristic of you, Martin, never to throw away anything that might come in handy later."

"Phin, you're insane. I'm supposed to have killed Danby, a perfect stranger. And I'm supposed to have killed Stokes, a man I never met at all! I suppose next you'll have me working with this Green, this Red spy or cat butcher or whatever he's supposed to be."

"No, you're not working with Green, you *are* Green. And, you know, this is the second time you've spoken of cats being butchered. You said before that—" Phin consulted his notebook—"that you couldn't believe the same person 'butchered a cat and then somehow killed Stokes', and so on. Odd, that. Because *only two living persons know how Stokes's cat died*. Me, because I found its corpse. And *Green*."

"Absurd! Aunt Dorothea knew, and so did everyone."

"No, Stokes only told her the cat was killed. She naturally assumed by poison, and that's what she told everyone. I never told any of you how the cat really died."

"You must be mistaken," said Martin quietly. "In any case, I can hardly be brought to trial on a chance choice of words, or even on having owned a rubber dinghy. You'll have to do better than that, Phin."

"Then I'd better begin at the beginning. Your building firm specializes in converting old houses into flats. Inevitably you met a few landlords who were anxious to be rid of sitting tenants —willing to pay anyone who could winkle them out. You took on the job."

Brenda said, "But he did charity work, visiting old people!"

"What better way to find new customers? Or rather, new victims. Every sitting tenant he found was a potential fee from a grateful landlord." He spoke to Martin. "You were an old hand at harassment by the time you started on Stokes. You knew enough to use a false name and take payments in cash, so the police couldn't find you—should anyone complain.

"Then came the bombshell. Stokes not only knew your Aunt Dorothea, he was going to visit her. He'd already phoned her to complain about this Green character. If he went to the reunion it would all come out."

"We've been over this before," said Martin. "I wasn't going to the reunion, I tell you! How could he see me there?"

"He wouldn't see you. He'd see what Miss Pharaoh kept on her mantelpiece—dozens of photographs of you. She was proud of you. She wanted to show off her prosperous nephew to her old friends. And with what result?

"At best, you'd be cut out of her will; at worst, you'd go to prison. Why take the chance, when it was so easy to kill Stokes and make it look as though he'd died naturally?

"Only it didn't quite work out. Miss Pharaoh had already hired me, and we became suspicious. You saw at once that there was only one permanent way to protect your inheritance—by claiming it. And from then on, *everything* you did was calculated to lead to the death of your Aunt Dorothea."

"Disgusting," said Martin. "You really think I'd kill a sick pensioner, and a blind man, and then the woman who raised me as her own child?"

"Disgusting, I agree, but I know you did just that. The first thing you had to do was set up the little colour-clue incidents, to distract attention from the name Green. And when you stole violets from your aunt's garden, you left a conspicuous false footprint. Anyone can pick up an old shoe somewhere and do the same."

Martin said, "What would be the point?"

"The point was to lead your aunt, step by step, to her own death. You knew she'd do exactly what she did: take that one positive-looking clue, and follow it wherever it led.

"It led first to Dawson, Sussex. Now that I think of it, I remember three points about that trip: Miss Pharaoh arranged it. She invited all the Unravellers. And she suggested we might take off our shoes and go wading. In retrospect, the reason is obvious: she'd brought along that plaster impression of a footprint, and she wanted to test everyone's shoes against it. I suppose it was in that hamper she kept fussing about?"

Portman snapped his fingers. "Of course! When we were all on the beach, and Latimer actually did go in wading, she asked Martin to run and fetch . . . and then said never mind. That could have been it."

Phin nodded. "The beach was too public. She wanted to go about her sleuthing in secret, before her quarry got rid of his incriminating shoes.

"But then we had another murder, and secrecy became impossible. And, Martin, *that* is what I really find disgusting. You had reasons for killing Stokes and your aunt—nasty reasons, but reasons. But you killed Danby for the most trivial, cold-blooded reason I've ever heard. You killed Danby to make it look like a pattern. You stuck a knife through him the way you stuck one through a Yellow Page—and with no more feeling."

Martin began to weep. "Cold-blooded? You're the cold-blooded bastard, sitting there saying . . ."

"Saying the truth!" A spasm of anger crossed Phin's mild features. "You may well weep, and I wish your tears were real."

Hyde saw that it was time to ask a question. "Tell me more about this 'pattern' business, Phin. I'm not clear on it."

Phin took a breath. "Well. We all saw how the colour clues made a pattern—the target for each clue was one of the Seven Unravellers. Martin saw a chance to make us see the same in his murder targets. It became a series, didn't it? After A and B, we expected C—and C was Miss Pharaoh."

"But he took a hell of a risk, didn't he?"

"Bigger than he thought. He couldn't know Sheila and Mia were listening. Had the house been empty, we'd never have found out when Danby was killed—or by whom. It was a gamble, and he just happened to lose. But not before murder C."

"He can't have killed Dorothea alone," said Portman. "No one could. And what about this accomplice—this mysterious stranger seen leaving her house?"

"His accomplice, yes: someone loyal, dedicated and completely trusting. I mean of course Miss Dorothea Pharaoh."

Phin produced the paper from Miss Pharaoh's desk and passed

it round. "When Miss Pharaoh wrote this, she supposed she was planning the strategy of her own investigations. In fact, she was giving the plan of her own murder. Notice first the peculiar references after each name: *wading*, meeting someone at 'j.r.' which we now know to be a *Japanese restaurant*, and finally a *sauna*. Notice that all these activities have one thing in common. *They are all occasions when one removes one's shoes.*

"I told you she was obsessed by that footprint. She planned, by one means or another, to get hold of the shoes of each of her fellow Unravellers. That of course explains her jokey title for this little plan: FOOTNOTES indeed.

"Now the reference for Leonard Latimer is more difficult to understand at first glance. She says 'The "Edom" plan (PS 60 8) using note to M., alice-door.' "

"Note to M.? That must be that note she sent to Martin, which none of us could understand," said Latimer. "But I don't see the rest of it."

"You will. What *was* the point of that note, anyway? Miss Pharaoh could have phoned it to Martin, or given it to him some other time. Why did she ask Sheila to drive all the way over to deliver it?

"The answer's simple, really. Sheila did not have to drive over to deliver a note—but she had to drive over to deliver a passenger."

"What's that?" said Portman. "Explain."

Phin turned to Sheila. "Remember when you last saw Miss Pharaoh? When she suddenly wanted you to make her a cup of cocoa and leave it outside her bedroom door?"

"Yes, she was all ready for bed—"

"Apparently. But we're not speaking here of a doddering old dear. We're speaking of a clever puzzle-maker, a keen amateur sleuth. She had no intention of going to bed with her supposed headache, nor drinking cocoa either. She had a dinner date with Gervase Hyde at a Japanese restaurant. Is that correct, Mr Hyde?"

"Yes. She said she might be a bit late."

"Because she had one other stop to make first. Sheila, Miss Pharaoh was wearing her nightie when you last saw her. But under it she already had on the trousers and boiled shirt of *her old dress suit*."

Hyde gave a yelp of laughter, then stifled it. "Yes, that's exactly what she would do. Trying to shock me, because she claimed I was unshockable. But you say it was her *old* suit? From the Unravellers?"

"She bragged," said Phin, "that she could still wear all her old clothes. Anyway, as soon as Sheila went down to the kitchen, Miss Pharaoh whipped off the nightie, put on her jacket, and hid her feminine hair under the only man's hat she owned. It's the old hat Martin bought her for gardening. What *size* was that hat, Martin?"

Martin had ceased glaring and weeping, and now looked simply pale with fear. "Size? I never noticed."

"Oh, you noticed all right. You took very careful note of that exceptionally small hat size, as we'll see." Phin stared at Martin for a moment before going on:

"She dressed, then, and slipped down and out of the house, carrying her precious plaster footprint in a shopping bag. She stowed away in the back of the car, and allowed Sheila to drive her to the Latimer house.

"While Sheila went in, Miss Pharaoh went round to the side of the house. Far back on the side, in the night shadows, there is a tiny private entrance for the Latimer cat. A little door which she calls in her notes the 'alice-door'. And there, with her plaster footprint impression, Miss Pharaoh waited.

"The rest depended upon her assistant inside the house. I said before that the *contents* of the note Sheila delivered were immaterial. It could as well have been a blank piece of paper. What mattered was the appearance of Sheila with the note. That was the signal.

"Miss Pharaoh's assistant was supposed to excuse himself, go into the passage to the cat door, and—"

"Wait a minute." Portman turned to Mrs Latimer. "I'd still like Mrs Latimer to explain what she was doing in that passage. Was she wiping blood off that golf club? Was she implicated in this plan or—?"

"*She?*" Mrs Latimer bristled. "You needn't talk about me as if I weren't here. I'll tell you what I was doing. I saw a spot of blood on the floor, where the cat must have dragged in another dead bird or something. I got a damp cloth and wiped it up, and then I happened to notice the cupboard door was ajar. I was afraid that animal had left something in there. So I opened it and looked. And that's all."

"You didn't touch the golf clubs?" Portman asked, crestfallen.

"I didn't even notice them. I was looking down at the floor, among the shoes."

"Among the *shoes.*" Phin paused for effect. "As I was about to explain, that was the task of Miss Pharaoh's 'inside man', to pass the shoes of Mr Latimer out through the cat door for her to compare them with the footprint.

"But it didn't work out that way. The assistant didn't bring out shoes, he brought out a golf club. He said something like, 'I'm having some trouble. Can you put your head in through the cat door for a moment?' Clever as she was, Miss Pharaoh trusted her assistant implicitly, so she obliged. He then struck her head with the club—nothing easier, he could even use a correct *stance*, for God's sake—and strangled her with her own bow-tie. It was all over in a minute or two. With the club, he pushed her head back out of the cat door. Then he cleaned the club and put it away, and returned to his backgammon game.

"He made minor mistakes, but they don't matter. Careless of him to miss a drop of blood on the floor by the cat door, but then how could he know it would be seen so quickly by the eagle eye of Mrs Latimer? By and large, this was a very professional job—just what we might expect from someone who's had a bit of practice."

Martin made a last feeble effort. "Have you finished your little charade? Because even if what you say is true, you haven't shown that *I'm* the assistant."

There was no humour in Phin's smile. "Not quite finished. You stayed till eleven to establish your alibi, then said good night. Outside you picked up the body and drove it to Miss Pharaoh's house, letting yourself in with her key. You carried her body upstairs and changed its clothes, removing the dress suit and putting on the nightie once more. The stud she had plucked from her shirt and clutched in a death grip—you could do nothing about that. The rest you bundled up with the plaster footprint and stuffed into a dustbin not far from Hyde's house. And that completed it, the 'charade' as you call it.

"And a charade is what it was: a carefully designed, engineered game, meant to mislead the innocent. With all her genius for playing word games and solving logic puzzles, Miss Pharaoh was naïve about the real world. She actually imagined that, with nothing but a bit of plaster and a trustworthy assistant, she could go sleuthing and find out a murderer. And you, the murderer, assisted her—step by false step.

"You've asked two questions: Is this a true account of what happened? And can I prove that you, Martin Hughes, were the murderous assistant?

"It is a true account. We can test this by trying to explain the facts by any *other* means. How else can we explain the 'mysterious stranger'? How else the shirt stud? How else the strangulation marks on the body's neck, which exactly match the stiff collar of her old suit? How else the forensic indications that the body was moved, some hours after death? How else the pointless note delivered by Sheila?

"And there is more to explain: the golf club used in this crime was found in the Latimer cupboard the next day. Only two persons could have brought it there from *outside* the house: Mr Latimer and Mr Hyde. But Mr Latimer was at home at the time of the murder, and Mr Hyde was in a Japanese restaurant—both surrounded by witnesses. Neither of them could have killed Miss Pharaoh at any place outside the Latimer home.

"But let's suppose an unknown accomplice did the deed, and that either Mr Latimer or Mr Hyde smuggled the golf club into that cupboard. Then we must believe either that Mr Latimer wants to incriminate himself—which the golf club almost did—or that either man lacks the common sense simply to dispose of the weapon as the clothes were disposed of, in a dustbin. That simple expedient would have made this crime utterly insoluble.

"Finally we must explain Miss Pharaoh's 'Footnotes'. They obviously refer to her plans for testing shoes against the casting." Phin read from the paper: "'Leonard's——the "Edom" plan (PS 60 8) using note to M., alice-door.' I've already given the explanation for this reference; the 'note to M.' and the 'alice-door' are clear. But what does 'Edom' mean? What is PS 60 8? I believe it can only refer to Psalm 60, verse 8: 'I will *cast out my shoe* over Edom.'"

Hyde groaned at the pun, then looked embarrassed.

"I believe," said Phin, "that answers your first question, Martin. Now we come to the second: Were you the assistant who murdered her?

"It must be the assistant who committed the murder, since no one else could possibly have known Miss Pharaoh was waiting outside the cat door. But who, at the Latimer house, could be that assistant?

"This is where an air-tight alibi can turn into an indictment. So long as we thought the murder took place at Miss Pharaoh's home, everyone in the Latimer house was above suspicion. But now that we know where and how she died, they are our entire set of suspects.

"The assistant cannot have been someone Miss Pharaoh suspected of murder. That rules out Portman, Latimer and Mrs Latimer. And since Miss Pharaoh thought Brenda *might* have killed Danby, it rules her out too. Mrs Portman, Garve and the Elliotts were strangers to her, so they're out. That leaves you, Martin.

"The assistant must be someone Miss Pharaoh trusted completely. Someone who knew all about the footprint casting, and perhaps had helped prepare the cast, and certainly someone who had helped lay plans for using it. Above all, he must be someone who knew that Miss Pharaoh's head was small enough to pass through the cat-door opening—who knew her size in hats because he had bought her a hat. Martin again.

"Finally, the murderous assistant must have gone into the passage *after* Sheila arrived with her signal, but *before* Mrs Latimer found a spot of blood on the floor. But everyone agrees that only one person went into that passage during that time interval: Martin Hughes.

"Any more questions?"

When Martin had been taken away, the others sat silent for a moment. A uniformed constable came down the slope, calling for Mr Phin.

"Yes, what is it?"

"There's a Mr Hodge here, sir. Says he's been trying to contact you for some time, about a rubber boat he's found in a canal somewhere. Says you promised a reward?"

"But how did he find me here?"

"He asked the police to find you. Seemed to think you were playing some sort of con-trick on him."

Phin smiled. "Tell him I'll be glad to pay him, but that he must turn in his evidence to you." He stood up, stretched and looked about him. Gervase Hyde was sitting very quietly.

"Don't start mourning," Phin advised. "I don't think she'd have wanted that. Sadness blurs the vision."

"Eh?"

Phin pointed his walking stick towards the House. "You might miss an interesting Surrealist landscape. Look at that!"

A helmeted policeman—a fat sergeant, in fact—was running pell-mell across the formal garden in pursuit of the half-inflated red and yellow balloon. The wind was dragging it away, and the Sheikh, in full white regalia, was trying to head it off from another direction. Suddenly the chase was joined by an old man, his beard flapping in the wind as he reached out for the object with his boat hook. But it escaped them all, slipping across the garden and finally coming to rest against a shrub. The shrub had been sculpted in the shape of an elephant.